M.C. Beaton (1936–2019) was the author of both the Agatha Raisin and Hamish Macbeth series, as well as numerous Regency romances. Her books have been translated into seventeen languages and have sold more than twenty-one million copies worldwide. She is consistently the most borrowed UK adult author in British libraries, and her Agatha Raisin books have been turned into a TV series on Sky.

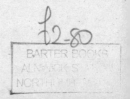

The Hamish Macbeth series

DEATH
OF AN
ADDICT

CONSTABLE

CONSTABLE

First published in the United States in 1999 by Grand Central Publishing,
a division of Hachette Book Group USA, Inc.

First published in Great Britain in 2009 by Robinson,
an imprint of Constable & Robinson Ltd.

This edition published in Great Britain in 2022 by Constable

1 3 5 7 9 10 8 6 4 2

A CIP catalogue record for this book
is available from the British Library.

ISBN: 978-1-47212-451-7

Typeset in Palatino by Photoprint
Printed and bound in Great Britain by Clays Ltd, Elcograf S.p.A.

Papers used by Constable are from well-managed forests and other
responsible sources.

Constable
An imprint of
Little, Brown Book Group
Carmelite House
50 Victoria Embankment
London EC4Y 0DZ

An Hachette UK Company
www.hachette.co.uk

www.littlebrown.co.uk

DEATH
OF AN
ADDICT

Chapter One

Shall man into the mystery of breath
From his quick breathing pulse a pathway spy?
Or learn the secret of the shrouded death.
By lifting up the lid of a white eye?
                    – George Meredith

Hamish Macbeth drove along a rutted single-track road on a fine September day. The mountains of Sutherland soared up to a pale blue sky. There had been weeks of heavy rain and everything seemed scrubbed clean and the air was heavy with the smell of pine and wild thyme.

It was a good day to be alive. In fact, for one lanky red-haired Highland policeman who had just discovered he was heart-whole again, it was heaven.

The once love of his life, Priscilla Halburton-Smythe, had been home to the Highlands on a brief visit. They had gone out for dinner together and his mind had probed his

1

treacherous heart but had found nothing stronger lurking in there but simple liking.

The sun was shining and somewhere out there were charming girls, beautiful girls, girls who would be only too happy to give their love and their lives to one Hamish Macbeth.

The vast heathery area of his beat which lay outside the village of Lochdubh had been crime-free, and so he had little to do but look after his small croft at the back of the police station, feed his sheep and hens, mooch around in his lazy way and dream of nothing in particular.

His beat had of late merely been a series of social calls – a cup of tea at some farm, a cup of coffee in some whitewashed little croft house. He was on his way to visit a crofter called Parry McSporran, who lived up in the wilderness of moorland near the source of the River Anstey, just outside the village of Glenanstey.

There are two types of Highlander, the entrepreneur and the cowboy. The entrepreneurs are hardworking, and set up schemes to earn money from tourists, and the cowboys are usually drunken louts, jealous of the entrepreneurs, and set out to sabotage their efforts. A taxi driver, for instance, who started to build up a successful business would suddenly find he was getting calls to pick up people in remote places and when he got there, he would find the call had been a hoax.

One who had started a trout farm found the water had been poisoned.

Parry McSporran had built three small holiday chalets on his land. During the building of them, he had experienced some trouble. Building materials had mysteriously gone missing; rude spray-painted graffiti desecrated his house walls.

Hamish had tracked down the youths who had done the damage and had threatened them with prison. After that Parry had been left in peace. He had recently started to take in long lets. He said this way he saved himself the bother of changing linen every week and cleaning the chalets. It was a good move, for the tourist season in Sutherland, that county which is as far north in mainland Britain as you can go, was very short.

Parry was moving his sheep from one field to the other when Hamish arrived. He waved. Hamish waved back and leaned against the fence to watch Parry's sheepdogs at work. There was nothing better, he reflected lazily, than watching a couple of excellent sheepdogs at work on this perfect day. All it would take to complete the bliss would be a cigarette. Stop that, he told his brain severely. He had given up smoking some time ago, but occasionally the craving for one would come unbidden, out of nowhere.

The transfer of the sheep being completed, Parry waved Hamish towards the croft house.

'Come ben,' he said. 'You are chust in time for the cup of tea.'

'Grand,' said Hamish, following him into the stone-flagged kitchen. Parry was not married. According to all reports, he had never wanted to get married. He was a small, wiry man with sandy hair and an elfin face with those light grey eyes which give little away, as if their bright intelligence masked any feeling lurking behind them in the same way that a man walking into a dim room after bright sunlight will not be able to distinguish the objects lying around.

'Got anyone for your chalets?' asked Hamish, sitting down at the kitchen table.

'I haff the two long lets,' said Parry, 'and the other one is booked up by families for the summer.'

'Who are your long lets?' asked Hamish as Parry lifted the kettle off the black top of the Raeburn stove which he kept burning, winter and summer.

'In number one is Felicity Maundy, English, Green.'

'You mean she's a virgin?'

'Come on, Hamish. Don't be daft. I mean one o' thae save-the-world Greens. She is worried about the global warmings.'

'In the Highlands!' exclaimed Hamish. 'A wee bit o' the global warming up here would chust be grand.'

'Aye, but she chust shakes her heid and says it's coming one day.'

He put a mug of tea in front of Hamish. 'Pretty?' asked Hamish.

'If you like that sort of thing.'

'What sort of thing?'

'Wispy hair, wispy clothes, big boots, no make-up.'

'And what is she doing up here in Glenanstey?' asked Hamish curiously.

'Herself is finding the quality of life.'

'Oh, one of those.'

'Aye, but she's been here three months now and seems happy enough. Writes poems.'

Hamish lost interest in Felicity. 'What about the other one?'

'Nice young man. Tommy Jarret. Early twenties. Writing a book.'

'Oh, aye,' said Hamish cynically. The ones who locked themselves away from civilization to write a book were usually the ones who couldn't write anywhere. 'Jarret,' he mused. 'That rings a bell.'

'Meaning he has a criminal record?'

'Probably not, Parry. I'll check into it if you like.'

'Aye, do that. I'd be grateful to ye, Hamish.'

'Mr McSporran,' called a soft voice from the open doorway. 'I wondered if I could buy some eggs from you.'

Hamish swung round. This, then, must be Felicity Maundy. The sunlight streaming in through the kitchen door shone through her thin Indian-style dress of fine patterned cotton and turned the wisps of her no-colour hair into an aureole. She moved forward into the shadow revealing herself to be a thin, young girl with a pale anxious face and nervous pale blue eyes which slid this way and that.

She was wearing a heavy string of amber beads which made her neck look fragile. Under the long skirts of her dress, she was wearing a pair of what looked like army boots.

'I'll get some for ye,' said Parry. 'Sit down. This here is Hamish Macbeth.'

Felicity nervously eyed Hamish's uniform. 'I'll just stand.' Her voice was as soft and insubstantial as her appearance.

'How do you pass the time up here, Miss Maundy?' asked Hamish.

'What do you mean?' There was now a shrill edge to her voice.

'I mean,' said Hamish patiently, 'it's a wee bit remote here. Don't you find it lonely?'

'Oh, not at all!' She spread her arms in a theatrical gesture. 'The hills and the birds are my companions.'

'Och,' snorted Parry, returning with a box of eggs, 'you should put on some make-up and heels and go down to Strathbane and have some fun.'

'I do not wear make-up,' said Felicity primly.

'Why not?' asked Parry. 'You could do with a wee bit o' colour in your face.'

'If one wears make-up,' declaimed Felicity as if reciting a well-rehearsed line, 'people cannot see the real you.'

'I shouldn't think anyone could see you, real or otherwise, hidden out here,' remarked Hamish.

Felicity ignored him.

'How much do I owe you for the eggs?'

'No charge today.'

'Oh, thank you. You are just too, too kind.'

Felicity whipped up the box and disappeared out of the kitchen door.

'That one's got you for a sucker,' remarked Hamish.

'Aw, she's chust the wee bit o' a thing. Needs building up. Will you check up on Tommy Jarret for me, Hamish?'

'I'll do it now,' said Hamish. 'Won't be a minute. I've got a phone in the car, although thae mobiles can be a pain. The number of places in the Highlands where they won't work!'

He went out to the police Land Rover and picked up his mobile phone and dialled police headquarters in Strathbane and got through to Jenny McSween, nicknamed the Keeper of the Records.

'Wait a minute, Hamish,' said Jenny. 'I'll just feed that name into the computer.'

Hamish leaned against the side of the Land Rover and waited, enjoying the feel of the sun on his face. The three holiday chalets were hidden behind screens of birch trees to give the occupants privacy. Through the flickering leaves of birch he could see Felicity's pale face at a window.

Then Jenny's voice came on the phone. 'Thomas Jarret, arrested last year, for possession of ecstasy and cannabis. Got off a pushing charge. Said they were for his own use and since only small amounts were found, he got away with it. Arresting detective, Jimmy Anderson, thinks he was pushing but couldn't make anything stick. Thomas Jarret was or is a heroin addict, you see.'

'I see,' said Hamish bleakly. 'Thanks, Jenny.'

He went back into the croft house and told Parry what he had learned.

'I'll haff that cheil out on his ear,' growled Parry. 'I cannae thole drugs.'

'Let's go and have a word with him,' said Hamish. 'He may be reformed. I'm all for giving folks a break.'

Parry, his face grim, walked ahead of Hamish and towards one of the chalets. He knocked at the door. 'Mr Jarret, we'll chust be having a wee word wi' ye.'

The door opened and a pleasant-looking young man stood there. He had a mop of curly brown hair and brown eyes in a tanned face. Those blinked rapidly when he saw Hamish's uniform.

'Can we come in?' asked Hamish.

'Y-yes.'

He backed away into the chalet living room. A word processor was on a table by the window, surrounded with piles of manuscript.

'Sit down,' said Tommy nervously.

'I'll get straight to the point,' said Hamish, sitting down and taking off his peaked cap and then twisting it round and round in his hands. 'You were arrested for possession of drugs. The arresting detective was convinced you were pushing.'

'I've been clean for six months. Honest,' pleaded Tommy. 'And I wasn't pushing. I went to a rehab in Strathbane. Ask anyone. In fact, I'm writing a book about my experience with drugs to warn other people what it's like.'

'Why were you found in possession of ecstasy and cannabis when you were a heroin addict?' asked Hamish.

Tommy gave a rueful smile. 'If you can't get your drug of choice, you'll go for anything.' He rolled up his shirtsleeves. 'Look, no track marks, and Mr McSporran here will tell you he's never seen me other than sober.'

'It iss not the drink I'm worried about,' said Parry.

'It's therapy-speak,' explained Hamish. 'Sober means he hasn't taken any mood-altering chemical. Am I right, Tommy?'

'Yes, I never even drink booze now. Please give me a chance,' said Tommy earnestly. 'You know I haven't been any trouble, Mr McSporran, and I pay my rent on time.'

'Aye, that's right,' said Parry reluctantly.

Hamish made up his mind. 'I'd let him be for the moment, Parry. I believe what he says.'

Outside in the sunlight, Parry said, 'You seem mighty sure of yourself, Hamish.'

'Like I said, I'm all for giving folks a chance. He seems a nice fellow to me. Come on, Parry. Strathbane's become a sink o' iniquity. I've seen a lot of good young people wrecked. This one seems to have pulled himself together.'

'I s'pose,' said Parry. 'He's no trouble. Let's hope your judgement is right, Hamish Macbeth.'

'Och, I am never wrong,' said Hamish with simple Highland vanity.

But when he had returned to Lochdubh and locked his hens away for the night, Hamish went into the police station office and phoned Detective Jimmy Anderson.

'Tommy Jarret?' said Jimmy in answer to Hamish's query. 'I mind him. Got away with possession and up in front of a lenient sheriff. Got nothing more than a stay in a rehab and a hundred days' community service.'

'Wait a bit,' said Hamish. 'He was a heroin addict?'

'Aye.'

'That's a pretty expensive drug to be taking

10

in the Highlands of Scotland. Where did he get the money?'

'Some aunt of his left him money, seems to be true. Respectable parents. Well off. Father a bank manager. Neat bungalow outside Strathbane, member of the Rotary Club, polishes the car on Sunday, get the picture? So he can afford heroin. I tell you another thing that made me mad. Couldn't get out of him where he got his supply from. I mean, he's lucky to be alive.'

'Why's that?'

'I believe there's a lot of adulterated stuff around and some bastard at the Three Bells pub down at the old docks was pushing talcum powder. The street price of heroin in Aberdeen was a hundred pounds per gram. Why are you asking about Tommy Jarret?'

'The name cropped up,' said Hamish.

'Meaning the wee bastard's in your parish. I don't trust any o' thae junkies.'

'Lot of drugs in Strathbane?' asked Hamish.

'Aye, it's a plague. It's the new motorways. We're no longer cut off up here so they zoom up the motorways from Glasgow and Manchester. The drug barons make money and more young people die every year.'

'What would happen, I wonder,' mused Hamish, 'if the stuff were legalized? I mean, there would be controls on the quality of the stuff and all the drug barons and drug cartels would be out of business.'

11

'Whit! It's statements like that which explain why you're a copper and I'm a detective. That's a load of dangerous rubbish you're talking, Hamish.'

'Just thought I would ask,' said Hamish meekly.

He rang off and then changed into his civilian clothes and went out for a stroll along the waterfront. He didn't mind at all being a mere village copper. Hamish Macbeth had sidestepped promotion to Strathbane several times. The waters of Lochdubh lay placid under a pale sky, with only the ripples from a porpoise to disturb the calm surface. The violent world of cities such as Strathbane seemed pleasingly remote.

'Dreaming, Hamish?'

Hamish, who had been leaning against the harbour wall, turned and found Dr Brodie's wife, Angela, surveying him with amusement.

'I was thinking of pretty much nothing,' said Hamish. 'Except maybe drugs.'

'I don't think we've got any cases in Lochdubh.'

'Good.'

She leaned against the harbour wall beside him and he turned back and rested his arms against the rough stone, still warm from the day's sunshine.

'Why do people take drugs, Angela?'

'Because they like the effect. You should

know a simple thing like that, Hamish. Then in the young, it's bad and exciting.'

'But all those warnings,' protested Hamish. 'All those kids dying from ecstasy pills.'

'Addicts never think it'll happen to them. And the young feel immortal anyway.'

'What if it were legalized?'

'I don't know. I don't think so. The illegality itself is a deterrent. Can you imagine if young people, children maybe, had unlimited access to LSD?'

'You're right,' said Hamish with a sigh. 'What's the solution?'

'Everyone starts refusing?'

'I cannae envisage that.'

'It could happen. Just become unfashionable. Like smoking. You're having a quiet time these days, Hamish.'

'Long may it last. I wouldnae like to see another murder in Lochdubh.'

'There may be one shortly.'

'Who? What?'

'Nessie and Jessie Currie are joint chairwomen of the Mothers' Union at the church this year.'

'Oh, dear.' Jessie and Nessie were middle-aged twin sisters, both unmarried.

'The others are complaining it's like being run by the Gestapo.'

'Can't they vote them out?'

'Not for another year.'

'What are they doing that's so bad?'

'Well, at the cake sale, they criticized the quality of the baking and reduced little Mrs McWhirter to tears, for one. Then they have lately become obsessed with germs and the church hall has to be regularly scrubbed. They have pinned up a cleaning rota and all women must remove their shoes before entering the hall.'

'I'll have a word with them.'

'Would you, Hamish? I don't know what you can say. Everyone's tried.'

'I'll have a go.'

Hamish said goodbye to her and strolled off in the direction of the Currie sisters' cottage.

He knocked at the highly polished brass lion's head on the door. Jessie answered, blinking up at him through her thick glasses. 'It's you. It's you,' said Jessie, who had an irritating way of repeating everything.

'I just dropped by for a wee word,' said Hamish easily.

'Come ben.' Hamish ducked his head and followed Jessie into the living room, where sister Nessie was seated.

Nessie was knitting ferociously, steel pins flashing through magenta wool.

'What brings you?' asked Nessie.

Hamish sat down. 'I'll get tea. I'll get tea,' said Jessie.

Hamish raised a hand. 'Not for me, thank you. This'll only take a minute.'

Jessie folded her arms and eyed the tall red-haired policeman nervously. 'It must be serious for you to refuse a free cup of tea, free cup of tea.'

'It iss the little matter o' the Mothers' Union.'

Nessie stopped knitting. 'What's up wi' the Mothers' Union?'

'The pair of you are what's up with it.'

'What d'ye mean, d'ye mean?' demanded Jessie. 'We run it wi' an iron hand, iron hand.'

'Well, now, ladies, the iron hand seems to be the trouble. Ye cannae go on like the Gestapo.'

'Who's complaining?' demanded Nessie wrathfully.

'Chust about everyone,' said Hamish Macbeth.

'We've done nothing wrong, nothing wrong,' said Jessie. 'We've made sure the church hall is clean, and that place was a sewer, a sewer.'

'Yes, and it iss the grand job the pair of you are doing at fighting the germs, but is there any need to fight the others?' Hamish reflected it was an odd world when the Mothers' Union was being run by two childless spinsters. Did anyone ever use the word 'spinster' any more? What was politically correct? 'Miz' was irritating and pretentious. Single? And why should women who were not married be considered strange in any way? He was not married himself.

'I'm speaking to you, Hamish Macbeth,' shouted Nessie, penetrating his thoughts, 'and all you can do is sit there like a gormless loon after insulting us.'

'Insulting us,' chorused Jessie.

'I wass thinking about Margaret Thatcher,' lied Hamish.

'What about her?' asked Nessie, a look of reverence in her eyes.

The sisters adored Margaret Thatcher.

'Well, now, Mrs Thatcher –'

'*Baroness* Thatcher,' corrected the Currie sisters in unison.

'Lady Thatcher, then. Now, herself would run that Mothers' Union with a firm hand. But she would delegate responsibility, draw everyone in. You get more out of people if they like you. Diplomacy is the word, ladies.'

'And what do you know about Lady Thatcher?' jeered Nessie.

Hamish half-closed his eyes. 'It wass the great day,' he crooned, his Highland accent becoming more sibilant as he worked himself up to telling one massive lie. 'I wass down in Inverness and there she wass, just doing her shopping like you or me.'

'When was this, when was this?' cried Jessie.

'Let me see, it would be June last year, a fine day, I 'member.'

'What was she buying?' asked Nessie, her eyes shining.

'It was in Marks and Spencer. She wass looking at one of thae tailored blouses she likes to wear. Silk, it was.'

'And did you speak to her?'

'I did that,' said Hamish.

'What did you say?'

'I asked her to autograph my notebook, which she did. I asked her the secret of success.'

Both sisters leaned forward. 'And she said?'

'She said the secret was the firm hand.'

'Ah!'

'But with kindness, she said. She wass as near to me as you are now. She said she never let herself get bogged down wi' bullying people or bothering about the small stuff. "If you work hard," she says to me, "you do the service for others chust because you want to. The minute you start pushing people and bragging about how hard you are working for them, they turn against you. Nobody wants a martyr."'

The sisters looked at each other. 'Maybe we have been a bit too strong, bit too strong,' said Jessie.

'Aye, maybe we'll go a bit easier,' said Nessie. 'And then what did she say?'

'Dennis, her husband, came up at that minute and he says, "You're neffer going to buy that blouse, Maggie. The colour's wrong." It wass the purple silk.'

17

'I'll bet she told him to take a running jump,' said Nessie.

'Not herself. She chust smiled and said, "Yes, dear, you're probably right." You see there wass the security men all about her and a lady like that wasn't going to stoop to be petty.'

'What a woman, what a woman,' breathed Jessie. 'We shall neffer see her like again.'

Hamish stood up, his red head almost brushing the low ceiling. 'I'll be on my way, ladies.'

'Can we see that autograph, Hamish?'

'Och, no, I sent it to my cousin Rory in New Hampshire. He has it framed and hung over his fireplace.'

Hamish made his way out. In the small hallway was a framed photograph of Margaret Thatcher. He winked at it and let himself out.

He ambled back towards the police station. As he approached Patel's, the general store, he recognized the waiflike figure of Felicity Maundy. In the same moment, she saw him and her face turned a muddy colour. She unlocked the door of an old Metro, threw her groceries on to the passenger seat, climbed in and drove off leaving a belch of exhaust hanging in the air.

'Now, what's she got on her conscience?' murmured Hamish. 'Probably went on some demo when she was a wee lassie at school and thinks the police still have a eye on her.'

18

He shrugged and proceeded along to the police station. His rambling roses at the front were still doing well and their blossoms almost hid the blue police lamp.

Hamish began to plan a relaxed evening, maybe put on a casserole and let it simmer and go to the pub for an hour. The new alcopops had turned out to be a menace, those sweet fizzy alcoholic drinks. They had been designed, in his opinion, to seduce the young, but it was the Highlanders, the fishermen in particular, every man of them having a sweet tooth, who had become hooked on them. So Hamish meant to combine pleasure and duty by keeping a sharp eye on the drivers who were drinking over the limit. Then he would return at closing time and start taking away car keys.

He opened the kitchen door and went in. The phone in the police station office began to ring shrilly. He went quickly to answer it. He experienced a blank feeling of dread and tried to shrug it off. It would be nothing more than a minor complaint. Or a hoax call.

He picked up the receiver. 'Lochdubh police,' he said.

'Hamish, this is Parry. It's yon fellow, Tommy Jarret. He's dead.'

'Dead. How? Why?'

'They think it's an overdose. They found a syringe.'

'I'll be right over.'

19

Cursing, Hamish rapidly changed into his uniform. How could it all have happened so quickly? he thought. The lad had been all right. What had happened to his, Hamish Macbeth's, famous intuition? He could have sworn Tommy Jarret was not in danger of returning to his drug taking.

He drove off up the winding road leading out of Lochdubh towards Glenanstey, his heart heavy. Large black clouds were building up behind the mountains. They seemed like black omens, harbingers of trouble to come.

Chapter Two

I will a round unvarnished'd tale deliver
Of my whole course of love; what drugs,
  what charms,
What conjuration, and what mighty magic,
For such proceedings I am charged withal.
                              – William Shakespeare

There is something particularly tragic about the death of a young person. Only that day, Tommy Jarret's life had seemed to stretch out in front of him. Now he was a crumpled piece of clay.

'You didn't touch anything?' Hamish asked Parry as they surveyed the body in silence.

'I checked his pulse. I had to make sure he was dead. Och, Hamish, he must have felt he was safe when you gave him that chance and so he decided to go back on the stuff.'

Hamish pushed back his peaked cap and scratched his fiery hair in bewilderment. 'But how did this happen so soon? How could it? Did he drive down to Strathbane?'

'I didn't see him go.'

'What about visitors? Where were you yourself this afternoon, Parry?'

'Here, now. You are neffer thinking I did it!'

'Come on, Parry. I want to know if you were around the croft. You might have seen someone or something.'

'I ran over to Dornoch to see about some spare parts for my car. I wass away the two hours.'

Hamish heard the wail of a police siren. 'That'll be Strathbane. I hope it's not Blair.' Detective Chief Inspector Blair was the bane of Hamish's normally quiet life.

But it was Blair's sidekick, Detective Jimmy Anderson, who came in. Policemen and a forensic team crowded in after him.

'No Blair?' asked Hamish.

Jimmy snorted with contempt. 'Blair wouldn't move his arse for a dead junkie.'

'Could be murder,' suggested Hamish.

'Oh, aye,' sneered Jimmy. 'The great detective has pronounced judgement. A junkie wi' a record is found dead with a syringe beside him and you ignore the obvious.'

'I was talking to him earlier today,' said Hamish stubbornly. 'And I could have sworn he would never go back on the stuff.'

'Let me tell you this, Hamish. Drugs is a dirty business. It gets them and it keeps them. Stuck up here in the backwoods wi' your sheep, you don't see much of life.'

The pathologist, Mr Sinclair, pushed his way past them. 'Give me some peace,' he said, 'until I have a look at this.'

Everyone walked outside. 'Now,' said Jimmy, turning to the crofter, 'you're Parry McSporran.'

'Aye.'

'Who's in the other chalets?'

'Only a wee lassie called Felicity Maundy.'

'Let's go and see her. May as well pass the time until Sinclair finishes and then the forensic boys will have to dust the place.'

At that moment Felicity came driving up. Her face turned white when she saw all the police cars.

She stopped and got out slowly. Hamish thought she looked as if she might faint.

'What do you know about this?' demanded Jimmy, advancing on her with a truculence worthy of his master, Blair.

She looked about her in a dazed way. 'Wh-what?'

'Tommy Jarret's dead.'

'He . . . he *can't* be.'

'It looks like an overdose.'

'But he was *clean*,' wailed Felicity, and then she began to cry.

'You'll get nothing out of her that way,' said Hamish. 'I'll get her a cup of tea. Come along, Miss Maundy. Time to have a word with you. We'll just go to your chalet and have a cup of tea.'

She was unresisting as he led her towards her chalet. 'Got the key?' he asked.

'I n-never bothered locking up.'

He opened the door and led her inside. Her chalet was identical to Tommy's except that dried herbs hung from hooks in the ceiling, there was a knitting machine in one corner and a sewing machine in the other. 'Now sit yourself down,' said Hamish soothingly.

He went into the small kitchen. There was nothing but herb tea so he made a cup of camomile and took it to her.

Hamish watched her as she sipped her tea and then said gently, 'Why were you so upset when you saw me outside Patel's today?'

'I didn't even see you,' she said, her eyes moving this way and that like a hunted animal.

'We'll leave that one for the moment. When did you last speak to Tommy?'

'Today. He asked me to get him some groceries from Patel's. He was working hard on his book.'

'How well did you know him?'

'Not very well. He was just a neighbour. He wouldn't have taken drugs.' She began to cry again.

Hamish saw a box of tissues on the kitchen counter and handed it to her. She blew her nose noisily. Hamish waited until she had recovered, thinking hard all the while. Why was she so shattered, so distressed, if she and Tommy had only been neighbours?

'And before you left,' he continued, 'did you see any strange people around? Hear a car?'

She shook her head. 'A couple of cars passed me on the road to Lochdubh heading the other way, but I didn't notice them particularly.'

'You must have noticed something about them,' said Hamish sharply. 'Colour? Large, small?'

She shook her head wearily. 'One was small and black, I think, and the other grey, and a bit bigger.'

'Hatchback? Saloon?'

'I don't know,' she wailed. 'And you're harassing me.'

Hamish decided to get back to her later. 'I'll send a policewoman to sit with you.'

He went out again and found a policewoman and directed her to Felicity. He approached Parry. 'What's the latest?'

'I heard thon pathologist say it's an open-and-shut case of an overdose.'

Hamish fretted because he felt he was being kept out of things. But, he reminded himself, it was his own fault for having decided to remain an ordinary copper instead of taking promotion when it had been offered.

After a long wait Jimmy Anderson, who had gone back into the dead man's chalet, emerged.

He came up to Hamish. 'They're taking the body away. They'll know more about what happened after a postmortem. But it all seems very straightforward. No murder for you, Hamish.'

'That book he was writing,' said Hamish. 'He was writing a book about his experience with drugs. Anything there? I mean anything that might have incriminated anyone?'

'We're looking into it,' said Jimmy sharply. 'Why don't you just get back to your beat and let us sort this out.'

'This is my beat,' said Hamish huffily.

'Aye, well, it's not as if you can do anything. Had the wee lassie anything to offer?'

'She said he was all right. She asked Tommy if he wanted any groceries, then she drove to Lochdubh. She said two cars passed her on the road going the other way but when I pressed her for a description, she started on about harassment, so I got out of there and sent in a policewoman.'

'If it was a murder case,' said Jimmy, 'she could howl about harassment until she was black in the face, but this is just an accidental death.'

'But Glenanstey is a dead end. After here the road doesnae go anywhere,' protested Hamish.

'Aye, but there's a wee road afore here that goes to Crask,' said Jimmy.

He walked off. Still Hamish waited until at

last the pathologist emerged and headed for his car. Hamish rushed over to him.

'What's the verdict?'

'Oh, it's yourself,' said Sinclair, the pathologist, sourly. 'It looks like an overdose. Anderson said he took heroin.'

'What's a lethal dose?' asked Hamish.

'In a non-tolerant person the estimated lethal dose of heroin may range from two hundred to five hundred milligrams, but addicts have tolerated doses as high as eighteen hundred milligrams without even being sick. But there's an odd thing about heroin addicts.' Dr Sinclair leaned his cadaverous body against his car and settled down to give a lecture. 'The reason for tolerance to heroin is partially conditioned by the environment where the drug was normally administered. If the drug is administered in a new setting, much of the conditioned tolerance will disappear and the addict will be more likely to overdose. Some pundits in the States believe that most of the OD cases are because of adulterated heroin. But oddly enough, British addicts who get clean heroin have about as high a mortality rate as Americans who shoot street crap. The health problems of addicts come from the use of needles, the presence of adulterants in the drug, the poor nutrition and health care associated with the hardcore addict –'

'Wait a bit,' Hamish interrupted. 'I saw Tommy today and he was healthy and happy.'

The pathologist sighed. 'Any addict is a tricky person. Very sneaky. He could have been talking to you and planning all the time in his brain when he was going to shoot up.'

'Could the dose have been forcibly injected?'

'There are no signs of violence or of forced entry to the chalet.'

'There wouldnae be any signs of forced entry. He probably kept his door unlocked day and night. I wonder about that book he was writing,' murmured Hamish. 'Oh, dear, I think that must be the boy's parents arriving.'

A stolid, middle-aged couple were getting out of a police car. The woman, plump and matronly, was weeping, her husband with the blank look of shock on his face.

Hamish said goodbye to the pathologist. There was nothing more he could do. But he took Parry aside.

'Look, Parry, Jimmy Anderson will get mad if I interfere but could you do me a wee favour? If you get a chance to speak to the parents – they'll be getting Tommy's effects – ask them if I could have a look at what he was writing.'

'I'll do that. Are you off then?'

'I'll just stop at the Irishman's cottage at the Crask turn. He might have seen some cars.'

Sean Fitzpatrick was a crusty old man. No one was quite sure when he had arrived from

Ireland, only that he was a retired builder. He had bought a ruin of a cottage and had restored it. The locals had tried to be friendly but as they said, 'Sean likes to keep himself to himself.'

Hamish had only exchanged a few 'good days' with the man but any attempt he had made to stop the police Land Rover and get out when he saw the old man working in his garden had resulted in Sean scuttling indoors.

He drove up, parked and got out. The sky was still brightly lit by a full moon. A thin thread of smoke was rising from the cottage chimney up to a black velvet sky where only a few faint stars glimmered. The black clouds he had seen earlier had retreated. The evening was cool and the air was sweet.

A deer, magnificently antlered, stood silhouetted on the crest of a hill above the little cottage with the moon behind it, as if posing for a photograph, and then disappeared with one long bound.

The peace of the evening entered Hamish's soul. He felt sure now that Tommy had indeed taken an overdose. It was his own vanity, he thought ruefully, that had made him want to find out if it was murder, because he had instinctively liked and trusted Tommy.

He opened the green-painted gate and walked up the short path and knocked at the door.

He waited patiently. At last the door opened a crack and an eye looked out at him.

'Police, Mr Fitzpatrick,' said Hamish. 'A wee word with you, please.'

The door opened wide. Sean Fitzpatrick was stooped and old but his eyes were bright and intelligent in his tanned and seamed face.

'What is it about?' he asked cautiously. He had a light pleasant Irish accent. Probably west coast, thought Hamish.

'It's about one of Parry McSporran's tenants. He's been found dead of a drug overdose.'

'And what has that to do with me?'

'Can I come in?'

'All right,' said Sean reluctantly. 'Just for a minute.'

Hamish tucked his cap under his arm, ducked his head under the low doorway and followed Sean inside, curious to see how this recluse lived.

Well, the answer is all here, thought Hamish, looking round the living room. Crammed bookshelves took up three walls, and beside the fireplace on the fourth was a CD player and neat stacks of CDs.

'Are these your company?' he asked, waving a hand to the bookshelves.

'Sure,' said Sean, settling into a battered armchair and indicating its twin opposite. 'But you didn't come here to talk about books.'

'Two cars going in the direction of Glenanstey were sighted this afternoon. Did you maybe happen to notice them?'

'At what time?'

Hamish thought hard. Felicity had arrived back at what time? Six o'clock. And he had seen her down at Patel's just before that. 'Say about five,' he said.

'I was in here listening to music,' said Sean. 'Didn't hear a thing. You know when I saw you, I thought for a moment you'd come about the monster.'

'Monster? The Loch Ness Monster?'

'No, there's a lot of fuss over at Loch Drim. Two of the women saw a monster. They phoned the police in Strathbane, but whoever they spoke to told them to go and have a cup of black coffee.'

'Why didn't they phone me?' asked Hamish crossly. 'Drim is on my beat.'

'Said it was too important for a local bobby to deal with.'

'And how do you know this? Folks say you never see anyone or go anywhere.'

'I go around to get my bit of shopping. Folks have a way of talking in front of me as if I'm deaf and invisible.'

'That's your own fault. You never talk to anyone.'

'I didn't retire to the Highlands of Scotland to talk to anybody.'

'Why did you come here? Where in Ireland are you from?'

31

'Mind your own business, Officer.'

'Well, if you can't help me,' said Hamish, rising and walking to the door, 'I'd better call over at Drim and take a look into this other business.'

Sean's eyes twinkled up at him.

'I think you'll find Jock Kennedy, who runs the general store, has thought up a way of drumming up business.'

'It would amaze me,' said Hamish bitterly, 'seeing how much they hate outsiders in Drim.'

Hamish was always puzzled that two such contrasting villages as Lochdubh and Drim could be situated on his beat. Lockdubh always seemed light and friendly. Drim was all that on the surface, but underneath there were black passions among the villagers, easily stirred up.

He thought that perhaps it had a lot to do with the location. It lay at the end of a black sea loch surrounded by towering mountains. It was almost as if the geography had made the people turn inwards upon themselves, suspicious of strangers, and anyone from outside was a stranger.

He drove down the twisting road to the village and parked outside Jock Kennedy's general store.

The shop was closed up for the night so he

knocked loudly at the side door which led to the Kennedys' flat over the store.

The burly figure of Jock Kennedy answered the door.

'What's all this about a monster?' asked Hamish.

Jock came out and closed the door behind him. 'Walk a bit with me, Hamish. I don't want Ailsa getting any more daft ideas.' Ailsa was his wife.

They walked down to the water's edge. Little waves rippled at their feet. A seagull called mournfully; in one of the cottages behind them, a woman admonished her child. Then there was silence, the silence of Sutherland, sometimes so complete it hurts modern ears.

Jock heaved a sigh, and then said, 'I don't want Ailsa or her friend Holly to be encouraged in this nonsense.'

'You'd best tell me what the nonsense is all about, Jock.'

'They were out walking along towards the sea.'

Hamish looked down at the black loch and then at the steep mountainsides which sloped straight down into the water.

'I've never been along there. I didn't know there was a path.'

'You cannae see it from here. It's little more than a rabbit track. Ailsa and Holly went out the other evening. They are both on some

33

exercise regime. They say just up almost at the head of the loch, they saw two great glaring green eyes staring at them out of some huge bulk in the water. It began to move silently towards them and they screamed and ran. Then they worked up all the other women in the village and reported it tae Strathbane police and were told to drink lots of black coffee. The police thought they'd been drinking hooch.'

'There's been a lot of Highland drunks recently reporting sightings of UFOs,' said Hamish. 'It was the bad time to call.'

'Anyway, I don't want them encouraged. There's a lot of phosphorescence in that loch and it produces queer effects.'

'I'll just take a stroll along there,' said Hamish. 'We'll let it drop for the moment, Jock, but if anyone else sees anything, there'll have to be a proper investigation.'

'Let's hope that'll be an end of it,' said Jock. Hamish touched his cap and made his way along the edge of the loch. He found the path at the westward end of the village. As Jock had said, it was little more than a rabbit track. He strolled along. He was glad he had brought his torch, the towering mountains made the blackness of the night even blacker.

He welcomed the exercise. He wanted something to take his mind away from Tommy. After a while, he could hear the waves breaking on rocks ahead. So it would be around

34

this point that Ailsa and Holly had seen their monster.

He swung his torch across the loch and let out a gasp as eyes stared straight back at him, eyes red in the torchlight. Then he laughed. Seals, nothing but seals. A whole colony of them. That must have been what Ailsa and Holly saw. He walked right to the sea, nonetheless, without coming across anything sinister.

His thoughts turned again to Tommy Jarret on the road back. It was a shame that one so young should have to die. But the more he thought about it, the more it seemed to him that the poor fellow *had* taken an overdose. Felicity had looked frightened at the sight of Hamish outside Patel's because she was an odd wispy creature who probably lived in some sort of private soap opera.

In the morning, he woke to marvel, not for the first time, at the mercurial changes the weather in the Highlands was capable of. Before he had gone to bed, the sky had been cloudless. Now it was raining steadily, with low clouds shrouding the tops of the mountains.

He did his chores about his croft at the back of the police station and then went indoors and changed into his uniform and phoned Strathbane police headquarters and asked to speak to Jimmy Anderson.

When Jimmy came on the line, Hamish asked if there had been any information from the pathologist. 'You're too early, too soon,' said Jimmy. 'Give the man a bit o' time. You're not still suspecting murder?'

'I reserve judgement,' said Hamish. 'What was in thon book he was writing?'

'I don't know.'

'What d'ye mean you don't know?' demanded Hamish sharply. 'He was writing about his experience with drugs. There could have been some useful names in there. I thought maybe you'd taken some pages away.'

'No, I didn't. Come on, Hamish. I grilled that bastard, 'member? Couldn't get the name of his suppliers out o' him. Why the hell would he put them in a book?'

'Just a thought,' said Hamish huffily.

'He died of an overdose, plain and simple.'

'While you're on the line, Jimmy, do you remember a couple of women in Drim reporting the sighting of a monster?'

'Not me. What are they up to in that nasty place? Trying to invent another Loch Ness Monster?'

'I shouldnae think so,' said Hamish. 'Do you 'member when that minister's wife and that television lassie produced that TV play featuring Drim? At first the tourists came in coachloads and the villagers didnae like it one bit. They even put a sign at the top of the road saying COACHES NOT WELCOME.'

'Hamish, between the drunks up in your part of the world and the druggies down here, we get reports of monsters and UFOs every week.'

'Just wondered.'

'Well, wonder away and go back to your sheep.'

Hamish said goodbye and then debated what to do. Then he decided to drive over to Glenanstey and have a word with Parry.

The birch trees around the chalet which Tommy had rented were weeping rainwater. Ferocious midges danced in and out of the raindrops. Hamish marvelled how the little beasts didn't get drowned. He knocked at Parry's door. There was no reply. He approached Tommy's chalet, wondering why there wasn't a policeman on duty. He tried the door and it opened. He went inside. Fingerprint dust was over everything. He stood in the doorway to the living room and looked around. The word processor stood on the table and beside it a small pile of typescript. He walked over and sat down at the table, took out a pair of thin gloves and put them on and began to read. Chapter one, which is all that there was, proved to be a disappointment. Tommy had meant his book to be an autobiography and the first chapter dealt with his school days. It was not very well written, the language being too flowery and loaded with similes.

He switched on the word processor and managed to find the beginning of the book. He ran through it. Only chapter one. Well, what had he expected? He had expected that Tommy had been killed because there was something incriminating in his manuscript.

He switched off the word processor and made sure that he had replaced the pages of manuscript exactly where he had found them.

Then he went outside and looked around. A policeman came up and stared at him suspiciously.

'I'm Hamish Macbeth from Lochdubh,' said Hamish easily.

'PC Peter Harvey,' said the policeman. 'I hope ye havenae been in there. I'm supposed to be guarding it. I just popped into the village for a cup of tea. It's a hell of a wet day.'

'So what's happening now?'

'Nothing much,' said Peter, lighting a cigarette. 'Strathbane says it's an overdose. The boy's parents will be along sometime to take away his stuff.'

'Do you know if they found any drugs in the chalet?'

'Aye, they found a wee bit o' heroin.'

'I'll just take a stroll into the village myself and have a cup of tea. Good idea. If you see Parry, tell him I'll be back.'

Hamish walked through the rain to the village, which consisted of a small huddle of houses. There was no shop, the locals all driving to Lochdubh to do their shopping. But there was a tearoom run by a Miss Black, an incomer, English. She had set up her tearoom in what had once been the village store. As she provided strong tea and very good cakes and biscuits, she had built up a regular trade among the locals as well as people in other towns and villages in Sutherland, many driving in from as far away as Lairg.

As Miss Black had bought the village shop for very little and acted as baker and waitress, a complete one-woman operation, she managed to make a modest living.

She was an energetic old lady. Gossip had it she was a retired schoolteacher. Unlike a lot of incomers, life in the northern Highlands of Scotland obviously suited her. Hamish judged her to be almost seventy but she had very good skin and pink cheeks. Her snowy white hair was arranged in a simple style. She wore an ankle-length tartan skirt, a tartan waistcoat and a white frilly blouse.

The café was empty. 'The weather's keeping everyone away but the police,' she said when Hamish walked in. 'What can I get you?'

'Tea and two of your scones and butter, please,' said Hamish, taking off his oilskin and hanging it on a hook by the door. 'Dreich weather.'

'It is, indeed. I gather you're here because of that poor young man.'

'Yes.'

'So sad. I'd never have thought he would do a thing like that and him so happy with his young lady.'

Hamish sat down at a table and looked at her curiously. 'I didn't know he had a young lady.'

'That little girl who lives at Parry's chalets. Felicity, that's it.'

'I was led to understand, I don't know why, that they weren't that close.'

'I thought they were in love, the way they were giggling and laughing together. Now, I'll get your tea.'

Felicity had definitely said that she didn't know Tommy very well, that they were just neighbours. Why had she lied?

A group of wet tourists came in, chattering and laughing. Miss Black served Hamish and then went to attend to them. He ate his scones and drank his tea.

Half his brain was yelling at him to leave well alone. It was an accidental death. But the other half was fretting about Felicity.

He finished, rose, nodded to Miss Black and went out again. A high wind had risen, and as he left the village and walked the short distance to Parry's, he saw that above the rain clouds were rolling back, like a curtain drawn back by a giant hand. By the time he turned in

40

at the gate of Parry's croft, sunlight was glittering on rainwashed grass and shining in puddles.

He waved to Peter, the policeman, and went straight to Felicity's chalet. The minute she opened the door to him and saw him, she began to cry. But Hamish felt there was something wrong, something stagy, about that crying. 'Just a few more questions,' he said.

She turned away and he followed her inside. She sat down, sniffling dismally into a tissue.

'Now, Miss Maundy,' said Hamish, removing his peaked cap and setting it on the table and taking off his wet oilskin, folding it and laying it on a bare bit of floor next to the fireplace, 'you told me that you and Tommy were just neighbours, nothing more, but I've been hearing reports that you were very close indeed.'

She took another tissue from the box and scrubbed her eyes and then stared at him defiantly. 'What if we were?'

'Nothing, but why did you lie?'

'Because you pigs always think the worst of everyone,' she spat out with sudden venom.

'Been in trouble with the police before?'

She stared at him mulishly.

He leaned forward. 'Look, Miss Maundy, all I'm trying to do is find out if Tommy just took an overdose. If you were fond of him, surely you'll want to help me find out about it.'

41

'I've been asked questions and questions,' said Felicity, 'and that detective told me it was a simple case of accidental death.'

The door opened and Peter, the policeman, walked in. 'A word wi' ye outside,' he said to Hamish.

Hamish followed him outside. 'I phoned Strathbane on my mobile to report in and said you was here asking questions. I've been told to tell you to go about your own duties. No point in having the two of us here.'

Hamish was almost glad that his mind had been made up for him. Forget about Tommy. Go back to a lazy, contented life.

'I'll just get my coat and hat,' he said.

'I didn't mean to get you into trouble,' said Peter.

'That's all right.' Hamish went back into Felicity's chalet. She was still sitting where he had left her. He picked up his oilskin and put on his cap. 'Good day to you, Miss Maundy.' He made his way out through the small kitchen. There was a selection of vegetables on the draining board; lettuce, carrots, mushrooms.

His Highland curiosity wouldn't even let the smallest thing go by.

'You a vegetarian?' he called.

The reaction was amazing. Felicity darted into the kitchen, her face flaming. 'Get out!' she screamed. 'Stop poking and nosing around!'

He shrugged. 'I'm going.'

Now what was that all about? he wondered as he walked to his Land Rover.

By a great effort of will, he convinced himself in the following days that poor Tommy's death had indeed been an accident. He went out on his rounds, a burglary over in Braikie took up some time, as did his chores about the croft. The days had stayed sunny, days to relax and breathe in some of the cleanest, balmiest air in the world.

A week after the death of Tommy, he drove back to the police station with the windows of the Land Rover open, whistling 'The Road to the Isles' and waving to people he knew.

And then a bright image of Tommy's young face rose in his mind. He whistled louder to banish it.

As he approached the police station, he could see two figures standing outside. As he drew nearer, with a sinking heart, he recognized Tommy Jarret's parents.

He parked the Land Rover and got out.

'We want to speak to you,' said Mr Jarret.

'Come into the station,' said Hamish. He opened the kitchen door. 'Would you like some tea?'

'No, thank you,' said Mr Jarret. 'What we have to say is very important.'

They both sat down at the kitchen table, the picture of middle-aged respectability.

Hamish sat down as well and said easily, 'How can I be of help?'

Mr Jarret took a deep breath.

'Our son was murdered and we want you to find out who did it.'

44

Chapter Three

I am . . . a mushroom
On whom the dew of heaven drops now and then.
— John Ford

Hamish leaned forward. 'You mean they found something in the pathologist's report other than heroin?'

'They found heroin, all right,' said Mr Jarret, 'but they also found traces of a strong sleeping drug. Don't you see? Someone must have drugged him, injected the heroin into him and made it look like an accidental overdose.'

'I thought there was something wrong about the whole business,' said Hamish. 'But surely the detectives in Strathbane are investigating the case. Why come to me?'

'Because they're not,' said Mr Jarret heavily. 'They say it was a simple drug overdose and they won't listen to us.'

'So how do they explain the presence of the sleeping drug?' demanded Hamish, exasperated.

45

'They say these drug addicts will take anything. They just don't want to know. That's why we came to you.'

'Why me?'

'I heard on the grapevine that you were clever, that you had solved cases and let your superiors take the credit. Justice must be done.' Mr Jarret clasped his hands tightly. 'I am prepared to pay you for your investigation.'

'That would not be necessary,' said Hamish, thinking hard. 'It will be difficult for me. I can keep on asking around. Tell me about Tommy.'

'He was so clever at school,' said Mrs Jarret, her eyes bright with unshed tears. 'We had great hopes of him. He was going to be an engineer. He went to Strathbane Technical College and the first year was fine. During his second year, that was when he started acting strange. He had been living at home, with us, but then he said he was moving out to a flat to share with two others.'

Hamish took out his notebook. 'What were their names?'

'We only ever heard their first names. Angus and Bob.'

'Address?'

'Number 244, Kinnock Tower, Glenfields Estate. We went there once. It was awful. Graffiti everywhere. And the smell! And the boys' flat was so bare. No furniture, only bedrolls on the floor. Not even a television!' Mrs Jarret looked at Hamish in a bewildered way, urging him to share her amazement at the oddity of a home without a television set.

'Give me a description of Bob and Angus.'

Mrs Jarret looked to her husband for help.

'Tommy said they were fellow students,' said Mr Jarret, 'but they didn't look like students to me. Although, mind you, I'm out of touch with modern youth. Angus was very tall, with straggly hair and a moustache. He wore jeans and a leather waistcoat over an undervest. No shirt.'

'No shirt,' echoed Mrs Jarret dismally.

'The other one, Bob, was small and fat and dirty. He had a shaven head and tattoos down his arms, small eyes and a sort of squashed nose.'

'Anything particular about the tattoos? Anchor, dragon, I Love Rosie?'

'There was a snake tattooed on one arm, a big snake which went round and round his arm.'

'Did Tommy ever bring them home to you?'

'Never,' said Mrs Jarret with a shudder. 'We tried to get Tommy to leave and come back home, but he said he was happy.' Her voice broke.

'He dropped out of college and out of our lives for a bit,' said her husband. 'Then the next thing we knew he was up on a drug charge. After that, things got better. He was so keen on writing this book, you see. He said that people thought they all knew what went on in the drug world, but they hadn't a clue. We said we would support him until the book was finished. It seemed so safe at that chalet he rented. McSporran seems a nice man, straight, no nonsense.'

'And what about his girlfriend?'

'Girlfriend?' Mr and Mrs Jarret looked puzzled.

'Felicity Maundy.'

Mrs Jarret's face cleared. 'Oh, that odd little girl who lives in the other chalet. He said she was just a neighbour, nothing romantic. She wrote us a very nice letter of sympathy.'

And yet, thought Hamish, the bright and intelligent Miss Black had said they seemed in love.

'About this book,' said Hamish instead. 'I had a look. It seemed to be a sort of auto-biography. There was only chapter one.'

'But that's the problem!' cried Mr Jarret. 'The last time we saw him, he said he was halfway through the book and there was a pile of pages on the table in the chalet the last time we visited him.'

'So what you think,' said Hamish, 'is that someone was frightened by what he was writing and they staged it so that it would look like an accidental overdose. Have you told the police this?'

'Yes, but they assured us we were wrong. That detective, Anderson, he said we were suffering from a reaction to the shock of

Tommy's death but that there was no mystery at all.'

'What about the sleeping pills? Did he take sleeping pills? What did his doctor say?'

'His doctor in Strathbane checked him into the rehab clinic but said he hadn't seen him since.'

Hamish leaned back in his chair and surveyed them thoughtfully. Then he said, 'It's a wee bit difficult. I do not have the resources of Strathbane, but I'll see what I can do.' He pushed over his notebook. 'Write down your address and phone numbers at which you can be reached.'

Mr Jarret wrote down their phone number, his business number and his mobile phone number. He raised weary eyes to Hamish. 'Does this mean you'll do it?'

'I'll do what I can,' said Hamish. 'Is there anything else you can think of?'

'He wouldn't have done anything to harm himself,' said Mrs Jarret. 'He believed in God.'

Hamish looked at her inquiringly.

'He even bought a Bible. He said God would stop him from taking drugs again. I would have liked that Bible.'

'You mean the police have still got it?'

'No, they said they had let us have all his effects.'

'Did he go to church? And if so, which denomination?'

'We're Church of Scotland. But I don't know which church he was going to.'

After the Jarrets had left, Hamish walked along to Dr Brodie's cottage.

'Come in,' said Angela with a smile of welcome. 'Did you say something to the Currie sisters?'

'Something.'

'Whatever it was, it seems to have worked. They're almost mild, for them.'

'I came to see your husband.'

'He's in the living room. Go through.'

The doctor was sitting in front of a messy smouldering fire. 'If you clean the ashpan out, it might burn better,' said Hamish.

'Oh, it's you, Hamish. Well, if you feel like cleaning it out, do it yourself.'

Hamish went back into the kitchen and collected the ash bucket. The doctor watched for a moment, amused, and then picked up the newspaper he had been reading. Hamish cleaned out the ash into the metal bucket and added several logs to the fire, which immediately sprang into life. He carried the bucket of smoking ashes out through the kitchen and placed them outside the kitchen door, then returned to the living room and sat down in an armchair opposite the doctor.

Dr Brodie put down the newspaper and

looked at Hamish over the tops of his spectacles.

'I'm sure you didn't call just to light the fire.'

'No, I've a bit of a problem,' said Hamish. 'It's that business about young Tommy Jarret.'

'Oh, sad business. Heroin overdose.'

'Aye, there may be a bit more to it than that.' Hamish told him about the visit from the Jarrets and their suspicions.

Dr Brodie listened carefully. Then he said, 'I see their point, but it's all a bit far-fetched for the Highlands of Scotland. It's natural in their grief that they should think up all sorts of conspiracy theories.'

'Well, I am not grieving, and I think it's all too pat. Did you prescribe sleeping pills for Tommy?'

'No. He registered with me when he moved to Parry's, but that was all. I don't have anything to do with drug addicts, Hamish, but the damn stuff creeps everywhere and I hope it never reaches up here.'

'It's a whole world I know nothing about,' said Hamish half to himself.

'I did hear from a colleague down in Strathbane, that there's a disco called Lachie's there. It's been raided several times but nothing has been found. Surely, Hamish, if Strathbane have decided it's an accidental death, then it must be.'

'Not necessarily. There's almost a sort of unholy glee when a drug addict dies. Silly bugger, he had what was coming to him. That sort of thing. Now, a lot of respectable businessmen, as you know, cause doctors and hospitals no end of expense and trouble with their drinking. But when one of them dies of a stroke or cirrhosis of the liver or pancreatitis, no one ever says he had what was coming to him. And drug deaths are often among the young and there's an awfy prejudice against young people.'

'But if you consider,' said the doctor, 'that there are warnings the whole time against the effects of drugs and no warnings against the effects of alcohol, other than the usual "don't drink and drive" warnings, people are apt to think, well, they were *told* what would happen. Like smokers.'

'Could be,' pointed out Hamish cynically, 'because the highest proportion of alcoholics are to be found amongst the medical profession.'

'Too true,' said Dr Brodie. 'Which reminds me, I got a present of a fine malt whisky. Fancy a dram?'

'Chust a wee one, then,' said Hamish, suddenly assailed by an odd nervousness. He knew that he should let Tommy Jarret's death go and not get under the feet of his superior officers. But at the same time, he knew that if he did not investigate it, that boy's death would nag at his conscience. While the doctor

52

went to fetch the whisky, Hamish wondered what to do next.

Felicity Maundy obviously knew something. Perhaps he would try her again. The following day was Sunday, his day off. He would put on plain clothes and see if that made him any less intimidating to her.

As he approached Sean's cottage, the following day, he saw the old man working in his garden and so drew to a halt outside the front gate and climbed down from the Land Rover.

'Morning, Mr Fitzpatrick,' said Hamish.

Sean straightened up from weeding and surveyed Hamish silently.

'It seems the monster in Loch Drim might be nothing more than seals.'

'How did you come to that conclusion?' Sean threw weeds into a bucket at his feet.

'I took a walk along the path that leads to the sea from Drim. There's a colony of seals on the rocks at the end.'

'That's odd,' said Sean. 'I thought there had been several sightings of something strange.'

'Oh, you know how it is here,' said Hamish easily. 'We pick up a good story and then we all embroider it.'

Sean shrugged and bent over his weeding again.

Hamish leaned on the garden fence and watched him. The day was milky grey and mild. It was very still, the sort of day where sounds carried from a long distance. It would be grand, he reflected, not to have to worry about the Jarrets, just let everything slide. Sean straightened up and surveyed Hamish with some impatience. 'Was there anything else, Officer?'

'You seem to hear a lot of gossip, although you keep yourself to yourself. Hear any more about the Jarret boy?'

'Nothing much.'

'Anything at all?'

'Only that he'd turned religious.'

'I heard a bit about that. Any idea if he went to church and if so which church?'

'Somebody said in my hearing it was some sort of odd religion that had started up in Strathbane.'

'The Moonies?'

'No, it wasn't them.'

'I'll look into it.'

'So you think it was murder, Officer?'

'Chust curious, that's all.'

Sean resumed his weeding and Hamish reluctantly got into the Land Rover again, reluctant because he was beginning to think that he would get no further with finding out what had happened to Tommy.

He drove on to Parry's croft and found the crofter at home. 'Felicity Maundy in her chalet?' asked Hamish.

'I don't think so. I think herself went out for a walk. Tea? Coffee?'

'Coffee would be fine.'

Parry picked up a battered enamel jug from the stove and poured two cups. Both men sat down at the table.

Hamish told Parry about Mr and Mrs Jarret's request. 'Do you really think there's anything mysterious about his death?' asked Parry.

'On a calm, still day like this, it all seems fantastic. But I won't be easy in my conscience until I've asked around a bit more. Now, this Felicity. She told me she was not that close to Tommy, they were just neighbours. But Miss Black, the woman who runs the village tea shop, she got the impression they were an item.'

'I can tell you, they weren't that casual, but I thought, both being young people stuck up here in the wilds, that they were just friends, Hamish. Went for long walks together, things like that. He could have been in her chalet at night, or her in his, and I wouldn't know. I'm dead to the world after ten o'clock at night.'

'So she lied, and what else has she been lying about? And then there's the book he was writing. His parents say he was half finished and yet all I could find was chapter one. Then there's the sleeping drug he had taken.'

'I didnae hear about that!'

55

'Aye, they found traces of some sort of sleeping drug. So, far-fetched as it may seem, someone might have laced his coffee and then injected him with heroin.'

'Okay, let's go for the far-fetched,' said Parry. 'In order to let someone into his chalet and, say, offer him coffee, it must have been someone he knew. Say someone he knew was a drug dealer and had mentioned in his book arrived on his doorstep, he'd have been frightened to death.'

'So what about Felicity?'

'Why her? She's chust a bit of a lass.' Parry's accent, like that of Hamish, grew more sibilant when he became excited or upset.

'I don't know,' sighed Hamish. 'I'm clutching at straws. Then there's this thing about him turning religious. Know anything about that, Parry?'

'We didn't talk much. No, I can't call to mind any sort of religious talk.'

'I'll try to find out from Jimmy Anderson if some weird cult has started up in Strathbane. He won't need to know I'm still investigating. I'll make it sound like idle curiosity.'

Parry glanced up at the window. 'There iss herself coming back after her walk.'

'Right,' said Hamish, getting to his feet. 'I'll have another wee word with her but I doubt I'll get very far.'

He walked next door to Felicity's chalet. The door was open and she was reaching up to take a cup down from a shelf in the kitchen. She turned and saw Hamish in the doorway. The cup fell from her fingers and smashed on the stone floor.

'I'm sorry I startled you,' said Hamish gently. He walked into the kitchen, saw a dust-pan and brush by the rubbish bin and, crouching down, neatly swept up the broken shards and put them in the bin.

'What do you want?' demanded Felicity shrilly.

'Now, then.' Hamish leaned against the kitchen counter. 'This is on my beat and I dropped by to see how you were.'

'I'm all right,' said Felicity defensively. 'If that's all, I have chores to do.'

'There's chust one thing I must ask you again,' said Hamish. 'Why did you tell me you and Tommy were only neighbours when from all reports you were closer than that?'

She was wearing a long gown of shimmery silk material of many colours. It made her look more waiflike than ever.

'Well, we were friends, yes, that was all. I thought you meant, were we having an affair?'

'Och, no,' said Hamish soothingly. 'Don't you find it lonely here?'

'No, I enjoy the peace of the countryside.'

'Do your parents support you?'

'I haven't seen my parents for a year. They're in Somerset.'

'So what do you do for money?'

57

'I'm on the dole.'

'I thought these days you had to get a job.'

'I'm a poet. There are no jobs for poets.'

'Neffer were, neffer will be,' said Hamish comfortably. 'Even Chaucer had a job.'

'There are not many jobs to be had in Strathbane that are suitable. I report every fortnight to the dole office to tell them I am still looking for work. What's it to you?'

'Curious, that's all. Was Tommy religious?'

'Like me, he led a spiritual life.'

'Whateffer that means. Did he go to church?'

'I really don't know,' she said, half turning away.

'You mean he didn't say anything on Sunday like, "I'm off to the kirk"?'

'We didn't live in each other's pockets. We respected each other's space. Now, if that is all . . .'

'Did he show you any of the book he was writing?'

She began to take carrots out of the vegetable basket and, turning on the cold tap, washed them.

'He said he would show it to me when he was finished.'

'And how much had he written?'

'How should I know?' she suddenly shouted. 'Am I under suspicion of anything?'

Hamish decided it was strategic to beat a hasty retreat before she threatened to report him to his superiors.

'I really chust called by to see that you were okay,' he said.

'I am. So goodbye.'

Hamish walked outside, looked around and wondered what to do next.

Then he decided to drive to Strathbane. He could take Jimmy Anderson out for a drink, if he wasn't out on some job. It was easy to get information out of Jimmy over a glass of whisky – provided Jimmy wasn't paying.

Hamish was in luck. Jimmy was not only at police headquarters but just finishing his shift. Soon they were seated in a nearby pub. Hamish had paid for two doubles.

'What brings you to Strathbane?'

'Day off. I thought I'd look at the shops. I've heard there's a good few open on the Sabbath.'

'There are that, but mostly the supermarkets and a few clothes shops. Everything else is closed down, just like the old days.'

'Someone was telling me something about some sort of religious cult that's started up in Strathbane.'

'Oh, them. Call themselves the Church of the Rising Sun.'

'Sounds a bit like a Rolling Stones record. What are they like?'

'Harmless bunch of freaks. Bearded men in sandals, dotty women. They'd got a shack of a place out on the north side.'

'And what do they do?'

'Bit like the Quakers. They wait until the spirit moves them and then they get to their feet and talk.'

'And who runs this place?'

'Chap called Barry Owen. English. No record. Sent a plainclothes along to one of their sessions. Said he was bored out of his mind. Why're you asking, Hamish?'

'Someone mentioned it. Just interested, that's all.'

'Anything happening up your way?'

'Nothing much. That fuss about some monster sighted in Loch Drim.'

'I told you. There's one daft report after another these days.'

Hamish looked at Jimmy's empty glass. 'Want another?'

'If you're paying.'

Hamish fetched another couple of doubles.

'I hear poor Tommy Jarret took some sort of sleeping drug afore he injected himself.'

'Where did you hear that?'

'The parents.'

'That poor couple plagued us with conspiracy theories about drug barons bumping their son off.'

'You must admit, the sleeping stuff looked funny.'

'Not to me. You don't have experience of junkies. They'll take anything.'

'So that's that.'

Jimmy looked at him narrowly, his foxy face suddenly alert. 'I should have known it wasnae just the pleasure of my company you wanted.'

'What gave you that idea? Just struck me as odd.'

'Junkies *are* odd, Hamish.'

They talked of general things and then Hamish took his leave. He drove out to the north side of Strathbane and stopped and asked several pedestrians until he had directions to the Church of the Rising Sun.

As Jimmy said, it was a shack, a wooden hut with a tin roof. A board outside in Gothic lettering proclaimed it to be the Church of the Rising Sun.

Hamish swung the police Land Rover around and parked it some distance away and then made his way back on foot.

As he approached the door of the building, there was such a silence that he thought there might be nobody inside. He tried the door and it opened. He blinked a little at the sight that met his eyes. About fifty men and women were sitting on the bare floorboards, facing a bearded man whom Hamish decided must be Barry Owen, the leader. Many of the congregation were in the lotus position. All were silent. Hamish sat down at the back of the group and waited.

Then one woman began to speak. She said she felt less than a woman because she could not achieve an orgasm. Then she fell silent. Another man began to speak. He spoke of his lusts, of his unfaithfulness to his wife. Hamish listened in amazement. It was more like a sex therapy group. Joss sticks were burning in old wine bottles at the corners of the room and the air was heavy with their smell.

After an hour of lurid revelations, Barry Owen got to his feet. He was wearing a denim shirt, jeans and trainers, no robes. He raised his arms. 'You have left all your troubles with me so they no longer exist. God be with you.'

And that was that. They all rose to their feet and made their way to the exit. One woman passed Hamish and he noticed that the pupils of her eyes looked unnaturally dilated. He had planned to interview Barry Owen when the 'service' was over, but he wondered rapidly whether he should pose as a new member of the congregation. From time to time his photo had been in the newspapers, but always just a small picture and in uniform.

He was still wondering what to do as he rose to his feet when Barry approached him.

'Welcome, brother.' He had a deep, sonorous voice.

'Welcome,' echoed Hamish.

'How did you hear of us?' asked Barry.

'Och, you know how it is,' said Hamish. 'I overheard someone talking about it.'

'And what troubles you, brother?'

'Maybe another time. I see folks are leaving.'

Barry put a hand on Hamish's shoulder and stared up into Hamish's hazel eyes. 'I am on call night and day. Speak, brother.'

'I don't think you can help me,' said Hamish. 'My troubles are not sexual.'

'We talk of other things,' said Barry. 'But most people are plagued with sins of the flesh.'

'I've often wondered why when anyone thinks of sin, they think of sex,' said Hamish, his treacherous Highland curiosity aroused. 'What about malicious gossip, ill will, unkindness?'

'You will find, brother, that all bad feelings stem from repressed sexuality.'

'But I'm not sexually repressed.'

'Ah, you think you are not, but excess of sex can in its way be a repression.'

Hamish was about to complain that he was hardly suffering from that either, but decided on the spot to become a member and see if there was even a smell of drugs about the place.

'I suffer from deep depression,' he lied. 'Sometimes I just don't want to get out o' bed in the mornings.'

'Ah, well, we must explore the root core of your depression. What is your job?'

'Nothing at the moment. I'm looking for one.'

Barry reached up and put an arm around Hamish's shoulders. 'There is a quality of innocence in you that I like. I tell you what, I

63

could do with a helper here. I cannot afford to pay you much.'

'What would my duties be?' asked Hamish.

'Cleaning up the place, helping to repair the fabric of the building. I would like the inside here painted green for a start. Green is a restful colour.'

Hamish's mind worked at great speed. He was due two weeks' leave. He could demand it immediately for family reasons. Sergeant McGregor at Cnothan could take over his beat.

'When would you like me to start?'

Barry beamed. 'Tomorrow is as good a time as any. Are you collecting the dole?'

'Yes.'

'Oh, well, go on collecting it and I'll pay you seventy pounds a week.'

'That's very kind of you,' said Hamish, privately thinking it was an encouraging sign of villainy that Barry should be prepared to cheat the government, forgetting that cheating the government out of its dues was considered in the Highlands as a legitimate occupation. 'Could you tell me when you started this . . . what is it, church or order or what?'

'I started a year ago. There's a wee room at the back. Come along and have a dram and I'll tell you about it.'

Hamish followed him through a door at the far end of the hall. It was a lean-to kitchen with a table and four hard chairs. Dirty dishes were piled up in the sink. Barry saw Hamish looking around and said, 'You can see why I need help. The place is a mess.'

'I thought some of your ladies might help.'

'Women, brother, women – these days we do not talk about ladies. They're all women and they are apt to get a crush on me.'

Poor souls, thought Hamish. He accepted a glass of whisky.

'I notice you did not take up a collection,' he said.

'We do that as they come in the door at the beginning. I teach them to have minds above material things and urge them to give generously. Money given to the church is never wasted.'

'So how did you get the idea?' asked Hamish, sipping his whisky and noticing it was a very expensive malt.

'God came to me,' said Barry, 'and He said to me, Barry, He said, there are folks out there with deep secret personal problems which are blocking the light of the spirit. Get them to come to you, urge them to talk so that their souls may be cleansed and let in the light of the spirit. I advertised in the local paper, people came along and I am building up a nice congregation.'

And probably a nice little moneymaker, thought Hamish cynically. It was amazing how people who claimed to have direct instructions from God always seemed to be justifying some selfish purpose.

'What time would you like me to start tomorrow?' he asked.

'About nine o'clock. You will find I am not very strict. Have you anywhere to live?'

'I've been sleeping in my car,' said Hamish.

'And yet you have kept yourself neat and clean. That says a lot for you. What is your name?'

'Hamish George.'

'Well, Hamish, there is a cot bed in the cupboard over there. I'll bring a pillow and a duvet. You can stay here for a bit. There's a stove there and coal and wood out the back.'

'That's very good of you,' said Hamish. 'Maybe my depression got worse because I had nowhere to live and no useful work.'

'Now you will be working for the Lord,' said Barry. Hamish's quick ear caught an almost mocking lilt in Barry's voice. Hamish had been bending his head in what he hoped was an attitude of grateful humility, but he looked up quickly. Barry looked back with an unctuous smile.

'Here's the key,' said Barry. 'It's a spare. I have things to do. I'll be on my way and leave you to lock up and fetch your things.'

Hamish waited until he had left and then he began to search the cupboards in the kitchen, under the sink, every nook and cranny, in the hope of finding a trace of drugs, but there was nothing. So here I am, he thought ruefully, wasting two good weeks' holiday working for a crackpot organization. Well, he could give it a few days and if nothing came of it, he could always go back on duty.

As a sign of his goodwill, he washed up all the dirty dishes and cleaned the stove before locking up and walking to his Land Rover.

He drove back to police headquarters and spun them a tale about an urgent family crisis. Then he headed out back through the town. There were several shops still open for business although it was Sunday. He stopped at a red traffic light and glanced idly out of the window. An expensive-looking boutique was open for business and in the window was a dress Hamish recognized. It was a twin of the one Felicity had been wearing when he had last seen her. The light turned to green. He drove round the corner and found a parking place and walked back to the boutique, which was called Lucille Modes.

He opened the door and went in. 'How much is thon dress in the window?' he asked. 'The silky one with the different colours.'

'One hundred and ninety pounds.'

Hamish blinked. 'That's a fair bit.'

The assistant said severely, 'It is pure silk and designed by Lucille herself. There is one on the rack over there.' She pointed. Hamish walked over and examined the dress. 'Do you make many of these?' he asked over his shoulder.

'Lucille made only three. People around here don't like to pay that much and then run into a lot of other people wearing the same dress,' said the assistant.

'It's a bit too much,' said Hamish, backing towards the doorway.

'Thought it would be,' said the assistant pertly.

Hamish drove thoughtfully back to Lochdubh. On his arrival, he mechanically went about his chores on the croft, made himself a simple meal, ate it and then sat down in the living room in his favourite armchair, clasped his hands behind his head and thought about Felicity.

How could she afford a dress like that? He went over every scrap of conversation he had had with her, how on the day of Tommy's death she had looked so frightened when she had seen him outside Patel's, then about how she had snapped at him that first time when he had looked at the vegetables on the draining board in the chalet kitchen.

He suddenly sat up straight. Mushrooms. What had he heard about mushrooms?

Angela Brodie was on the Internet and seemed able to conjure up reams of information.

He hurried out and along to the doctor's cottage. Angela answered the door.

'This a social call, Hamish?'

'No, I'm after some information about mushrooms.'

'What kind?'

'The druggie kind.'

'Come in. I think they're called shrooms. I'll see what I can get for you. Go in and take a seat and wait.'

Hamish went into the living room. There was no sign of the doctor. Must be out on a call.

He sat down and picked up the day's papers, which he had not read.

After half an hour, Angela came in and handed him a printed sheet. 'That's what I got, Hamish.'

The page was headed 'Liberty Cap/Magic Mushroom, Psilocybe semilanceata'. There was an illustration of some spindly mushrooms. The liberty cap's habitat appeared to be in grass, fields, heaths and meadows. Season was given as late August to mid-January. Colour: buff when dry, brown with bluey tinge when wet. Thin black lines can also be seen through the lower margin when wet.

Then came the comments. 'Psilocybe semilanceata has been used for thousands of years and is probably the most well known and most used psychedelic mushroom in the UK. The usual number of mushrooms ingested is between 25 and 50. Effects are similar to many of the psychedelics but often without the harshness and intensity that is associated with

LSD. The effects come on between 10 and 40 minutes after ingestion and last approximately 3 to 4 hours. Eating fresh magic mushrooms is legal in the UK.'

Hamish put down the printed sheet and said half to himself, 'If it's legal, why was she so afraid of me?'

'What's this about?' asked Angela.

'These magic mushrooms. I think that wee lassie Felicity Maundy may have been peddling them.'

'They grow pretty much everywhere, Hamish. She wouldn't get much for them. She'd get more from growing cannabis.'

'I tell you, Angela, she was wearing a dress and I saw the twin o' that dress in Strathbane and it cost a hundred and ninety pounds and yet herself said she was on the dole.'

Angela looked at him thoughtfully. Then she said, 'Well, maybe sweet little Felicity was peddling something else.'

Hamish thanked her and went back to the police station. How could a mushroom which caused a psychedelic effect lasting up to four hours be legal?

He phoned Strathbane. Jimmy Anderson was at home but when Hamish volunteered that he wanted to ask someone about drugs he was told that Detective Constable Sanders had just come in and was their expert.

Hamish introduced himself and then asked why shrooms, or magic mushrooms, were legal.

'Ah, but they're not really,' said Sanders. 'You pick them, that's legal. You prepare them, dry them, make tea from them, then it's illegal. It's illegal to change them in any way so I suppose you can say that someone picking them was actually changing them.'

Hamish thought about the mushrooms he had seen on Felicity's draining board. They certainly had been small-capped and with thin stems.

'Would anyone get much for selling them?' he asked.

'Not that I've heard. People mostly pick them for their own use. Mind you, we raided a house last year after a tip-off and the attic floor was covered in those mushrooms.'

'I wondered if you ever heard of anything against a young English lassie called Felicity Maundy.'

Sanders's voice sharpened. 'You mean the one that lives next door to Tommy Jarret?'

'Don't be telling anyone I asked,' said Hamish, alarmed. 'I'm told the case is closed.'

'Look, I'm going off duty. Do you mind if I pop over to Lochdubh for a wee word?'

'Not at all,' said Hamish. 'I'll be waiting.'

Chapter Four

'One side of what? The other side of what?'
thought Alice to herself.
'Of the mushroom,' said the Caterpillar,
just as if she had asked it aloud; and in
another moment it was out of sight.

– Lewis Carroll

Detective Constable Sanders had sounded brisk and intelligent on the phone. Hamish imagined him as being tall, dark and with severe features.

He was surprised when he opened the door some time later to what at first in the darkness looked like little more than a schoolboy.

'Sanders,' announced the detective.

'Come in,' said Hamish.

In the bright light of the kitchen, Sanders turned out to be a fairly small man with a thatch of thick blond hair, a boyish fair face with a snub nose covered in freckles and bright blue eyes.

'You look too healthy to be a drug expert,' said Hamish.

'Well, I don't take the stuff myself.' Sanders sounded amused. 'So you're the infamous Hamish Macbeth.'

'Take off your coat and sit down,' said Hamish. 'Tea? Coffee?'

'Coffee would be grand. Dash of milk, no sugar.'

When they were seated over their coffee mugs, Sanders said, 'We meet at last. I've heard a lot about you.' He held out his hand. 'I'm Joe.'

Hamish shook it.

'So, Joe, what brings you all this way?'

'It's the Tommy Jarret business. I wasn't satisfied.'

'I wasn't either and I still am not,' said Hamish.

'Tell me why.'

'I think you had better tell me your reasons first. I don't want to get into trouble.'

Sanders laughed. 'Meaning you want to know if you can trust me? Here goes. I think the case was closed quickly on Tommy because he had a record, because he took drugs. There was a general feeling that he was asking for it, that one less junkie in Strathbane can only be good. It was the pathology report that bothered me first. Do you know there were traces of a sleeping drug in the body?'

Hamish nodded.

'Then there was that book he was writing. It all seemed too neat and easy that only chapter one detailing his early life should be found. Then there was the matter of fingerprints.'

'You mean there were no fingerprints!'

'I'm not saying that. There were Tommy's, Parry McSporran's and Felicity's. But the door handle was wiped clean.'

'The outside door?'

'Yes.'

'But Parry found the body. Surely his prints would have been on the handle?'

'Parry said the door was wide open and he walked in. He said the bedroom door was open as well.'

'Why did Parry go in? I forgot to ask him.'

'He said he saw the front door wide open and walked across to make sure Tommy was at home. Parry said that although nobody locks their doors up there, he thought if Tommy had gone out and left the door open, it was tempting someone to steal his word processor.'

Hamish leaned forward eagerly. 'But footprints!'

'Now here we come to the real mystery,' said Sanders. 'From the bedroom through to the outside, the floor had been wiped clean and there was a mop propped outside the chalet without a fingerprint on it.'

'Then they can't say the case is closed!' cried Hamish.

'They have and it is. So what's your interest?'

Hamish decided to trust him. He told Sanders all about the visit from Tommy's parents, about Felicity and the dress and what he suspected about the mushrooms.

'But if she was messing with magic mushrooms,' finished Hamish, 'they would have found something when they searched her chalet.'

Sanders remained silent, looking down into his mug of coffee.

'Neffer say they didnae search her chalet!' exclaimed Hamish.

Sanders raised his eyes. 'No, they didn't. But acting on your information, I can organize a raid and let you know if we find anything. We'll check her bank account as well, see if she's been banking any unusual sums of money.'

'There's one thing I didnae tell ye,' said Hamish. He described his visit to the Church of the Rising Sun and how he had taken leave to work there because it looked like Tommy had been a member.

Sanders began to laugh again. 'Now I know why Blair calls you the worst headache in the police force. Man, what if you're recognized?'

'I'll take that risk.'

'I'll get news to you somehow. I've always thought there was something wrong about that church. Now, I'd better go and get some sleep before I raid Felicity's place tomorrow.'

'And I'd better go and borrow an old car from someone,' said Hamish. 'I'm supposed to have been sleeping in my car because I'm one of the homeless.'

'You know that recluse Sean Fitzpatrick, who lives out on the Crask turn?'

'Aye.'

'He bought a new car last year. His old one is round the back. It may still be working. He's like a crofter. They never throw an old car away, just keep it in the garden for spares.'

'I'll try him now.'

'It's nearly midnight.'

'He's old. He's probably still awake.'

Sure enough, when Hamish parked outside Sean Fitzpatrick's, he saw the lights were still on. He knocked at the cottage door and after a few moments, Sean answered it.

He sighed when he saw Hamish. 'The reason I get the reputation of being a recluse,' he growled, 'is because I am one. So leave me alone.'

'I chust wanted to know if I could rent your old car out the back.'

'What for?'

'I've got two weeks' break and them in Strathbane don't like me driving around the police Land Rover.'

77

'It's not insured.'

'I'll get it insured,' lied Hamish.

'I've a feeling the only way I'm going to get rid of you is to let you have it. Wait and I'll get the keys and we'll see if it starts.'

He reappeared with the keys and they walked round to the back of the house, Sean carrying a torch. 'That's it,' he said.

It was an old Volvo, one of those large ones built like an undertaker's hearse. It was rusted and dirty.

Sean got into the driving seat and turned the key. The old car roared into life. He backed it out on to a heathery track that ran down the side of the cottage.

'I'll charge you twenty-five pounds a week and I want it back with a full tank of petrol,' said Sean, getting out.

'Thanks,' said Hamish.

'And I'll be having the first twenty-five now.'

Hamish fished out his wallet in the lights of the car. A solitary five-pound note stared up at him.

'I haven't the money on me.'

'A cheque will do.'

Hamish got out his chequebook and wrote a cheque out, leaning on the bonnet.

'There you are,' he said, handing it over.

'Fine. I'll just write the number of your bank card on the back.'

'I'm a policeman,' said Hamish huffily. 'You ought to trust me.'

'From what I've heard, you're a permanently broke policeman. Card, please.'

Hamish handed it over. 'Hold the torch for me,' said Sean.

Hamish shone the torch while Sean carefully copied out the bank card number on the back of the cheque.

'Fine,' said Sean. 'Take care of it. It's a good car.'

Hamish looked moodily at the dirty, rusty car. 'You'll get it back in the same grand condition you're letting me have it,' he said bitterly.

He drove back to Lochdubh and before he went to bed, he packed up the back of the Volvo with a bag of clothes and then spread out an old quilt and a pillow to make it look as if he had been sleeping in it.

He then set the alarm before he went to bed. In the morning, he would start his new job. And before that, he'd better stop off at the doctor's and beg Angela to look after his sheep and hens while he was away.

Joe Sanders had hoped to raid Felicity's chalet as early as possible in the morning but he found he had to cut through a lot of resistance and red tape before he got the necessary search warrant.

It was nearly midday when, flanked by a policewoman and a policeman, he arrived at Felicity's chalet.

To his relief, she was at home. When he held up the search warrant, she looked as if she might faint. He began the search. Neither kitchen, living room nor bedroom yielded anything. Another dead end, he thought, and wondered briefly how Hamish was getting along.

Hamish had been doing very well. The old Volvo was very convincing, he thought. He started the painting job. He was up a ladder, whistling to himself and reflecting that painting walls was a relief after police work, when he felt himself observed.

He looked down. Barry Owen was standing there and beside him was a hard-faced woman with flaming-red hair which owed all to art and nothing to nature. She had a stocky, muscular figure encased in a pink track suit which clashed horribly with the colour of her hair.

Barry called up. 'The wife and I are stepping out for a moment. I'll introduce you when I get back.'

Hamish swore under his breath as his eyes met the hard suspicious eyes of Mrs Owen.

Parry appeared in the doorway of Felicity's chalet. 'What's going on here?' he asked.

'I have a search warrant,' said Sanders. Parry could see behind him the small figure of Felicity slumped at the kitchen table.

'Find anything?' he asked.

'Nothing in the kitchen, bedroom or living room. There's nowhere else. We're just finishing up.'

'Nothing in the upstairs room?' asked Parry.

Felicity began to cry. Sanders ignored her.

'What upstairs room?'

'I'll show you.'

Parry led the way into the bedroom and pointed to the ceiling which had been covered with an Indian curtain. 'Up there is a trapdoor. I made a spare room upstairs.'

'Where's the ladder?'

'It's in this cupboard.'

Parry opened a cupboard and brought out a folding steel ladder. Sanders opened it up, mounted it and then tore the curtain away from the ceiling and dropped it on the floor. He raised the trapdoor and looked around and then smiled. The whole of the floor of the room was covered in mushrooms, drying out, piles and piles of liberty caps – magic mushrooms.

He climbed back down, grinning in triumph. 'She's got enough magic mushrooms up there to send the whole of Strathbane on a trip!'

Barry Owen and his wife, Dominica, walked a little away from the church. 'Where did you find him?' Dominica jerked her thumb back at the church.

'He turned up yesterday at the service,' said Barry. 'I had a word with him. He was sleeping in his car. I offered him the job of painting and caretaking.'

'God, you're naive,' sneered Dominica. 'I go away for a few days and you risk taking on someone we know nothing about.'

'I am a good judge of character,' said Barry huffily, unconsciously echoing Hamish Macbeth.

'I tell you what we are going to do.' said Dominica. 'We're going back in there and you will get him down from that ladder and I will speak to him . . . alone.'

Barry shrugged. 'I've got to go down into the town anyway. You'll find he's harmless.'

'Hey, you up there!'

Hamish looked down. Dominica Owen was standing there, her hands on her hips, glaring up at him.

'What iss it?' he asked, his accent made sibilant by nerves.

'I want a word with you.'

Hamish reluctantly placed the paintbrush on top of the pot of paint, which was balanced on a cross beam, and slowly made his way down the steps. He followed her through to the kitchen.

'Sit down,' she commanded.

He sat down at the kitchen table and looked at her meekly.

'Who are you?' she demanded.

'Hamish George.'

'And you are unemployed?'

'Yes.'

'But you must have worked at some time?'

'Crofting. I wass a shepherd.'

'So what happened?'

'I got a bit funny and low in my head. I couldnae get out o' bed in the morning.'

'Who were you a shepherd for?'

Hamish suddenly clutched her hand between his own. 'You must help me,' he wailed.

'What with?' she demanded in an exasperated voice, and tried to drag her hand away, but he had it in a strong grip

'With the black devils that come into my brain,' said Hamish. 'You must exercise them.'

She succeeded in snatching her hand away. 'Exorcise, you village idiot,' she corrected.

Dominica looked at Hamish in distaste. A thin trail of spittle was running from a corner of his mouth down his chin.

'You're drooling,' she said sharply, and Hamish muttered, 'Sorry,' and wiped his chin with the back of his hand.

'You will need to speak to my husband about your devils,' she said, getting to her feet. 'Get back to work.'

Hamish gave her a vacant look and shambled off.

'Trust you to employ the village idiot,' she said to her husband later. 'There must be a lot of inbreeding in the Highlands and Islands. Oh, well, he seems harmless enough.'

Sanders was determined to get something out of Felicity Maundy. A charge for possession of the mushrooms, he knew, would probably get her a suspended sentence.

She had screamed and cried and protested and called him 'fascist pig', but now she was silent and mulish.

He wondered briefly if she had an eating disorder. Her wrists and ankles looked thin and fragile. Or, he then wondered cynically, did she go out of her way to cultivate a waif-like image as a shell of protection?

He returned to the attack. 'You told PC Macbeth that your income was from the dole.'

Silence.

'Answer me!' Sanders thumped the table between them in exasperation.

'Yes,' she whispered.

'Louder. For the tape.'

'*Yes!*' she shouted.

'And yet according to your bank, a regular monthly sum of eight hundred pounds is paid into your account. The cheque comes from a Mr James Maundy. Your father?'

'You have no right to poke your nose into my affairs,' she hissed.

Sanders sighed. 'Don't you see? You are a very silly girl. You wear expensive clothes. Where did you get the money? If we had not found out your father was sending you a generous allowance, we would have assumed that you had got the money pushing drugs, hard drugs, for you won't get much for your bloody, stupid mushrooms. Still, I may as well ask. Have you been pushing drugs?'

'No!'

'Very well, then. Let's discuss the death of Tommy Jarret.'

He noticed the sudden stillness, the rigidity of her body. He suddenly decided to take a chance, although he cursed the running tape and the presence of the policewoman behind him. What he was about to do could get him into serious trouble. He could only be glad about one small thing. She had not asked for a lawyer.

He leaned forward and stared straight into her eyes. 'We know you killed Tommy Jarret,' he said.

He fully expected her to shout another no, and then to threaten to call down the wrath of the authorities on his head.

But she began to shake and tremble. 'I didn't mean to,' she said, and then she began to weep, great tears coursing down her face.

He handed her a box of tissues and waited, suppressing a rising feeling of excitement. When she had calmed down slightly, he said soothingly, 'You'll feel better if you let it all out. What happened?'

She continued to gulp and sob for what seemed to Sanders a long, long time. Then she dried her eyes and said in a dry whisper, 'I didn't mean to.'

'Tell me about it.'

'Tommy told me he had been going to this church in Strathbane.'

'The Church of the Rising Sun?'

'Yes. He said Barry Owen, the preacher, was very spiritual. Tommy said he still often had a terrible craving for heroin, but that Barry had told him that if he got in touch with God, then he would be able to fight the craving. He . . . he told me, he felt so *earthbound*, that although he believed in God, he could not get a *sense* of God. I . . . told him, I told him about the mushrooms, and about how they made things of the spirit so tangible.'

She hung her head.

'So you encouraged him to go on a mushroom trip. When was that?'

'The day before he died.' She raised pleading eyes. 'Don't you see? I started him on the road back to drugs. I didn't mean to. I really didn't mean to. I didn't think I had done any damage. He told me he should never have taken the mushrooms. He said he never wanted to take any form of drug again, and I heard that pathologist say that one drug leads to another . . .'

For the first time, Sanders realized he was listening to the truth. And all she had said only went to confirm the idea that Tommy had gone back on heroin and overdosed. He had known reformed alcoholics hit the bottle again because they had taken a liqueur chocolate or some of Auntie's sherry trifle.

And it seemed as if the Church of the Rising Sun might be nothing more sinister than some sort of minor scam to dupe money out of the gullible.

Hamish Macbeth may as well chuck in his job and save the rest of his holidays for something better.

Hamish, meanwhile, had discovered that there were services every weekday evening between six and seven. Barry urged him to attend.

'I'll be there, but I don't have sexual problems,' said Hamish.

'But you see,' said Barry eagerly, 'although sex, I believe, is at the root of our problems, we share our other troubles. People take the subject from the person who speaks first. So you must speak of your depression and others will follow your lead.'

Hamish was sitting on the floor at the back of the hall that evening, waiting for the service, if it could be called that, to begin. There were fewer people than on Sunday, only about twenty-five. Just as Barry made his entrance from the kitchen to stand in front of them, Hamish sensed someone sitting down next to him and glanced sideways. Sanders!

'Now,' began Barry, raising his arms in a sort of benediction, 'before we begin, I must thank you all for your generosity But –' he held up the collection box – 'I am sad to say that some of you are not giving freely. To get in touch with God, you must cast aside material things. We will pray together and then the collection box will be passed among you for further contributions.

'Dear God, soften the hearts of your people so that they may give generously. You, dear Lord, know the paucity of the collection and you frown and your wrath is terrible.'

Hamish switched his mind away from the prayer and wondered instead what Sanders had found out to bring him to the church. Then there were those two supposed students Tommy had lodged with. He had their names and address in his notebook. Maybe go into town after the service and after he had heard what Sanders had to say. His thoughts ran busily on until the prayer was finished and the collection box came round again. He noticed a woman putting a twenty-pound note into it. When it came to him, he put in a pound. Barry would not expect him to afford any more. He was not paid until the end of the week.

He was looking up towards the ceiling and

admiring the start of his paintwork when he became aware his name was being called.

'Hamish!'

Hamish started and looked at Barry Owen. 'Come forward, brother,' commanded Barry.

Feeling every bit the idiot Mrs Owen believed him to be, Hamish went forward. He stood with his shoulders hunched and a vacant smile on his face. Then he saw that Mrs Owen was not in the congregation and decided it would not be politic to act the empty-headed fool too much, as he had not pulled that act on Barry.

'Now, brother,' said Barry, 'tell us your troubles.'

'I suffer from depression,' mumbled Hamish, seeing a mocking grin on Sanders's face.

'Louder. The Lord must hear you!'

'I suffer from depression,' shouted Hamish, thoroughly embarrassed. 'Och, I cannae talk about it in front of all these people.'

'You will, when the spirit of the Lord enters you.' Barry reached up and laid his hands on Hamish's head. Hamish felt a shock like an electric current running through his body.

The superstitious Highland part of his mind wondered if Barry really did have healing powers. The police side wondered what electrical device Barry had hidden in the palm of his hand.

'Go and join your brothers and sisters and listen to their help,' said Barry.

Hamish thankfully hurried back to his place next to Sanders.

One by one, various members began to talk about how depressed they had been until they had joined the church.

Then to Hamish's amazement, Sanders leapt to his feet. 'I had been a sufferer from chronic depression for years,' he said, 'until the light entered my soul.'

'Hallelujah,' shouted a thin woman, clutching a shopping bag on her lap.

'And do you know why?' he shouted.

'Tell us!' urged the congregation.

'My sexual orientation was wrong, wrong, *wrong*.'

'Ah!' A sigh of satisfaction came from the congregation. Back to good old sex at last.

'I was locked in an unhappy marriage. I could not bring myself to touch her. She repulsed me. I prayed to the Lord. My brain cleared. I was gay. I would not admit that before, even to myself. My black cloud lifted and I saw the light.' Sanders smiled fondly down at Hamish, who glared at him.

'My brother here will come with me and I will explain in private how he might be helped.' He stretched down his hand. 'Come, brother Hamish.'

'Yes, go,' cried the congregation in a state of ecstasy.

Blushing as red as his hair, Hamish allowed Sanders to lead him out of the church.

'Well, hello, sailor,' said Hamish bitterly.

'How else was I to get a private word with you?' said Sanders.

'So you can let go of my hand.'

'Such a nice hand,' said Sanders, patting it. 'You should see your face.'

'How did you know they would just let me walk out with you?' asked Hamish.

'Easy. I'd dropped in there before, under-cover. Sex, always sex. They wank off just talking about it. So I knew if I got them back on their usual track, they wouldn't mind.'

'So what's this all about?' asked Hamish. 'How did you get on with Felicity?'

Sanders told him as they walked down towards the town.

Hamish felt depressed. 'So all that does is add evidence to the fact that Tommy did kill himself by accident.'

'Looks that way, and I think you're wasting time in that damn church.'

'Maybe something there,' said Hamish. 'Maybe they show blue films?'

'So what? Have you seen television lately? Even the BBC shows everyone screwing every-thing. Turn to the nature programmes for a bit of relief, and they've got animals shagging.'

'Are you gay?' asked Hamish abruptly. 'Not that it matters. I'm just curious to learn if the hidebound dinosaurs of Strathbane police have moved into the twentieth century.'

'No, but it was the best thing I could think of to get you out of there.'

'So what now?' asked Hamish. 'I suppose that's that. I might have a go at just one more lead.'

'What's that?'

Hamish told him about the two supposed students that Tommy had lodged with.

'I doubt if you'll find them still there,' said Sanders. 'Worth a try all the same.'

Hamish looked at him sharply. 'You mean you still think there was something funny about Tommy's death?'

'Yes. It's a gut feeling.'

'So are you going to come with me to see these two former friends of Tommy's?'

'No, I go on a lot of drug raids. They might be a couple I busted.'

'Then what about the people in the church, for heaven's sake?'

'I checked them out as they went in. Nothing sinister there.'

'Oh, my,' moaned Hamish. 'I'm working at that church for nothing.'

'You mean they aren't paying you?'

'Aye, they're paying me, and I better look noble if I stay to the end of the week and put the money in the collection box because if headquarters gets a wind of me taking money, I'll be out on my ear.'

'I'll leave you here,' said Sanders, stopping by his car. 'I parked well away from the church.'

'It's an ordinary car, not a police car,' said Hamish. 'Why did you do that?'

'I wanted to go on foot for a bit. Gave me a better chance to suss out the people going into the church. Are you going to see these blokes in your capacity as police officer?'

'No.'

'Well, you look a damn sight too clean. Take my advice and muck yourself up a bit. And let me know if you even get a whisper.' He took out his notebook. 'I'll write down my home address and number. You may get into trouble.' He tore off the piece of paper and handed it to Hamish.

Hamish waved to him and walked off into the night.

What a smelly place Strathbane was, he reflected as he headed down to the old docks where he knew Glenfields housing estate to be. Smells of gas and sour earth and cheap cooking.

He wished he hadn't shaved that morning. He wished he hadn't pressed his shirt. He was too old to pose as a student.

He walked through the estate until he found Kinnock Tower. The lift wasn't working. Wearily he began to climb the stairs. The walls of the staircase were covered in graffiti and the stairs themselves in rubbish. The whole estate had been due for demolition for some time but kept being put off, because temporary accommodation would have to be found for the inhabitants and then new houses built and there was no money for that, perhaps because the councillors of Strathbane had a propensity to travel to exotic places en masse on 'fact-finding' missions, and taking their wives with them, and all at the taxpayers' expense.

The flat he was looking for was near the top of the building. He trudged along until he came to 244. A blast of stereo sound came through the thin door. He rang the bell, and then, reflecting that the bell probably didn't work, knocked at the glass panel of the door, which had been broken at one time and stuck together again with sticky tape. Still no reply. He bent down and shouted through the letter box, 'Anybody home?'

The door was suddenly jerked open.

A small, fat, piggy man stood there. He was bare to the waist. A snake was tattooed around one arm. Bob, thought Hamish.

Bob's eyes dropped to Hamish's feet. Hamish was glad he had put on an old pair of trainers instead of his regulation boots, which he often wore even when he was in plain clothes.

'Whit d'ye want?' demanded Bob.

Hamish leaned indolently against the door jamb. 'I heard I could get some good stuff here.'

Bob thrust past him and peered up and down. 'Come in,' he said.

The outside door opened straight into a

living room. The noise from the stereo was so loud it seemed to make the thin walls vibrate. There was little furniture, beanbags on the floor, one with a knife slash in it and the contents spilling out on to the bare boards. The room was littered with empty Diet Coke cans. Hamish had never seen so many.

'Wait here,' said Bob.

He went into another room. There came sounds of an altercation. Then silence. Then Bob came back, followed by a tall young man with long unkempt hair and a straggly moustache. Angus, thought Hamish.

'What stuff?' demanded Angus.

'Heroin,' said Hamish.

'Oh, yeah? What makes you think we've got any drugs.'

'You haven't,' said Hamish insolently. 'Not in the quantity I need to buy.'

Hamish knew impersonation came better from the inside. His very sneering insolence, the contempt in his eyes as he looked them up and down, he knew was a better disguise than if he had tried to dress up in the character of a drug baron.

'How much are we talking about here?' demanded Angus.

'Fifty thousand pounds for starters.'

'Whit! Show us the money.'

'Do you think I'd bring that much into a slum like this?' Hamish's eyes raked over the mess of the room. 'I'm moving business to

Strathbane and someone told me you two knew the drug scene.'

'Oh, aye? And just who would that someone be?' demanded Bob, who had taken out a large knife and was waving it about.

'Put that bread knife away, you silly wee man,' said Hamish.

'Who're you calling a silly wee man?' roared Bob. 'I'll cut your face.'

Hamish stared at him unmovingly.

'Put the blade down,' snapped Angus. 'So, big man,' he said to Hamish, 'which syndicate are you from?'

'As if I would tell you,' jeered Hamish. 'Just get me in touch and there's money in it for you.'

'How much money are we talking about?'

'A hundred for each of you. You get me the contact and you get your money.'

'Where do we get in touch?'

'You don't. Name a place and time and I'll be there.'

'Wait a bit.' Angus jerked his head at Bob and both went into the other room and shut the door behind them.

When they had gone, Hamish forced himself to maintain his role of big-time drug dealer. He knew if he relaxed the act for one moment, he would feel frightened and the fright would show.

There was an opened packet of cigarettes lying among the debris of Coke cans and half-eaten food in a corner of the floor. He stared at it hungrily, all the old longing for a cigarette flooding his body.

But just when he felt himself weakening, the door opened and Bob and Angus came back in.

'Took your time, didn't you?' demanded Hamish.

'Lachie's. Do you know Lachie's?'

'The disco.'

'That's the one. Be there Thursday at nine o'clock.'

'Okay. I'll be seeing you.'

Hamish walked quickly to the door, nodded to them and walked outside, shutting it firmly behind him. He then stood a little way away from the door so that his silhouette could not be seen against the frosted glass and listened. 'Follow him,' he heard Angus say.

Hamish took off like a hare, running lightly on his trainers. He darted down the stairs and then along a corridor leading to the flats below. He pressed against the wall and waited until he heard Bob clattering down the stairs in pursuit. He waited until Bob's footsteps had faded away and then he made his way leisurely down the stairs, his mind in a turmoil.

What had he done? How on earth could he follow it through? What on earth had possessed him?

He would need to get hold of Sanders fast.

* * *

He made his way cautiously along the dark empty night-time streets, always listening for the sound of pursuit. In the centre of the town, he found a phone box and dialled Sanders's number.

'Hamish,' said Sanders crossly. 'What now?'

'I need to see you. Now,' said Hamish. 'I'm in a mess.'

'Okay, come round. Get to police headquarters, go on along Strathie Street past four turnings on the left going north, and the fifth is Tummock Drive.'

'I'll be as fast as I can,' said Hamish, and rang off.

Sanders listened to Hamish in silence and then said, 'There's two things you can do, Hamish. One, go back to Lochdubh and forget about the whole thing. Two, come with me to police headquarters and let's see if we can follow this through.'

'Blair will have my guts for garters.'

'Blair's away for a week. Superintendent Daviot'll need to be in on this. You'd better stay the night and come in with me in the morning.'

Wondering what they were making of his absence from the church, Hamish endured the wrath of Jimmy Anderson the next morning.

Anderson howled that Hamish had lost his mind. Sanders said quietly that they had never really nailed a good drug bust and if Hamish could lead them to where the supplies were coming in, it would be a marvellous coup. Jimmy Anderson sourly said they should put the whole matter before Chief Superintendent Daviot. Hamish endured another gruelling session and then was told to go back to the church and maintain his cover until they got in touch with him. Until then, he was not to be seen at police headquarters again.

'Where the hell have you been?' demanded Barry when Hamish arrived looking haggard and unshaven.

'I talked most of the night with that fellow. He wass most helpful.'

'I'm docking the time from your wages,' said Barry. 'Get to it. Any more days off and you're finished here.'

Tired as he was, Hamish was glad of the work to take his mind off his troubles. He had gone to see Bob and Angus with no clear idea of what to say. Whatever had possessed him not only to tell that monstrous lie, but to say that he could come up with fifty thousand pounds?

He worked until just before the evening service was due to take place and put away his paint pots and soaked his brushes and then got in Sean's old car and drove to Lochdubh. After he had soaked in a hot bath and changed his clothes, he began to feel better. He had not been fired. As he had pointed out, he was doing the investigation in his own free time. They could either go ahead with it or tell him to stop being a maverick and never, ever do anything like that again without consulting his superiors.

There was a knock at the door. It was Angela, the doctor's wife. 'Your sheep are all right and your hens are fed and locked up for the night.'

'Thank you,' said Hamish. 'Come in.'

'I can't. I'm rushing. You look awful. Been out on the town?'

'Aye, you could say that,' said Hamish.

After he had said goodbye to her, he locked up the police station and drove off towards Strathbane. It was a cold, crisp night and great stars blazed overhead. He drove steadily until he saw the orange blot on the sky which meant he was approaching Strathbane.

He parked outside the church and walked around the back to the kitchen door. There were lights on in the kitchen. He stopped and then went forward softly and put his ear to the kitchen door.

Barry's voice sounded sharp and clear. 'Betty Jones hasn't paid up. She's in arrears.'

'Then take her pension book,' came his wife's voice.

'She won't give it up.'

'Threatened her with the wrath of God, did you?' sneered his wife.

'Didn't have the slightest effect. She says she can't pay.'

'We need some muscle on this. Trust you to employ a halfwit.'

'I wanted the church painted,' said Barry peevishly. 'We employ muscle, we'll have to pay for it.'

Hamish drew softly away from the door. So the Owens were loan sharks, using the church as a front. Lend money at high interest and if they didn't pay, take their pension book or dole payment book. He was about to retreat and go back to police headquarters and report what he had heard. But he had been told to stay at his job at the church until he was contacted.

He went back to the car, let in the brake and cruised down the hill a little without switching on the engine. Then he switched it on and turned and drove back up to the church, revving the engine before he stopped and this time getting out and slamming the door loudly. Then he walked up to the kitchen door, whistling loudly, and opened it.

The Owens were sitting there over cups of coffee. Mrs Owen had a large bag at her feet which she zipped shut when Hamish walked in. No doubt where she had shoved the books, thought Hamish.

'Come in, lad, and the Lord be with you,' said Barry unctuously. 'We were just leaving.'

Hamish tried to look as vacant-eyed as possible until they had gone, for Dominica kept throwing him nasty little looks.

At least he had something on them. How horrible they were! Now all he had to do was wait until headquarters managed to get in touch with him.

He was working busily on Wednesday, wondering all the while if the powers that be had decided to let the whole thing drop. It was a blustery, windy day and he had left the church door standing open to dry the paint. He had reached ground level on one of the walls and was bending down to fill in a bit he had missed when his sixth sense told him he was being watched.

He straightened up slowly and turned round. A woman of about his own age, thirty-something, stood there. She had thick black hair tied at the nape of her neck with a black ribbon. She was wearing a tailored suit and flat shoes. She had an oval face, large brown eyes and a generous mouth.

'What can I do for you?' asked Hamish.

The woman looked around. 'Can we get out of here for a bit? We need to talk somewhere private.'

Hamish glanced at his watch. 'It's just about lunchtime.'

'Then we'll have lunch.'

They walked a good bit away from the church before she stopped by a small car. 'Get in,' she said, 'and we'll go into the centre of town.'

They had driven a few streets when she said, 'I gather you will have guessed I am here to brief you.'

'Are you somebody's secretary?'

'I am Detective Inspector Chater.'

'Sorry, ma'am.'

'And that was a sexist remark if ever there was one.'

'This,' said Hamish, waving an expansive hand, 'is sexist country. You cannae be from Strathbane.'

'I have been brought up from Glasgow. Don't talk until I negotiate this bloody awful one-way system.'

She parked at last in the private car park of the Grand Hotel. Any hotel called the Grand conjures up visions of Victorian or Edwardian elegance, but this one was pure Strathbane: a square, modern building decorated in the height of geek-chic, plastic and vulgar and pretentious.

The dining room was fairly empty. She demanded, and got, a table in a secluded corner.

They ordered from a huge menu filled with glorious descriptions of crackling this and fresh that, and sizzling the other. Hamish ordered fish and chips – 'Sea-fresh haddock in golden crispy batter and pommes frites' – and she ordered steak and a baked potato – 'Prime cut of Angus with floury baked potato and lashings of fresh Scottish butter.'

Detective Inspector Chater surveyed Hamish curiously. 'You are a little better than I expected.'

'What did you expect?'

'You don't look as stupid as I expected.'

Hamish raised his eyebrows

She clasped neat little hands with well-manicured and unpolished nails on the table.

'These are the facts as they were given to me. You suspect there is something fishy in the death of a junkie, even though it seems a perfectly straightforward overdose. So you take leave, take a job in some weird church and then go calling on two of the dead man's former flatmates. Once there, for God knows what mad reason, you pose as a drug baron and say you've got fifty thousand pounds to pay for heroin. Instead of sticking a knife in you or saying they didn't know what you were talking about, this unlovely pair – we've checked on them – who do not even have a record, promptly play your game.' Her eyes took in his outfit of old sweater, frayed shirt and paint-stained trousers. 'My guess is that they were playing games with you. How on earth could anyone take you for a drug baron?'

Hamish leaned back in his chair and his face suddenly became a mask of sneering arrogant insolence and his eyes stone-hard. 'Why not?' he drawled.

'If you looked like that, they might just have fallen for it, but I doubt it. Anyway, I've been dragged up from Glasgow to play this comedy through to the end.'

'Have you got the money?' asked Hamish.

'No, I haven't got the money. Are you mad? We both go to Lachie's for the meet and take it from there. What we want to find out is not if Lachie is dealing but where the supplies come in. The west coast of Scotland is such a maze of sea lochs and creeks, it could be anywhere.'

'And who are you supposed to be?'

She gave a little sigh. 'I am supposed to be your wife. They've got a house for us.'

'And who are we?'

'I will give you the big names in one of the main Glasgow syndicates and brief you on what to say. You are Hamish George – I believe that's the name you were using at the church.'

'How did you know that?'

'We have our methods, Watson.'

'I'll need to know your first name. I cannae call you ma'am the whole time.'

'It's Olivia.'

Hamish smiled. 'A pretty name.'

'Don't get any ideas, Constable, and remember at all times when we are not on the job that I am your superior officer.'

'Yes, ma'am,' said Hamish meekly.

'You may as well start calling me Olivia and get into the act. Here's our food.'

Hamish picked away at a truly dreadful plate of fish and chips while Olivia sawed her way through a tough steak.

'Tell me, ma'am,' he said. 'I mean Olivia, are you going to be dressed like that?'

'No, I shall look the part. What about you?'

'I've got a good suit,' said Hamish proudly, who had bought a Savile Row one in a charity shop.

'We'll lend you some accessories. A gold Rolex, few bits like that.'

'I'll go home this evening and get my suit.'

'That's the last time you'll go near that police station of yours until this is all over. What will you tell them at the church?'

'I don't need to tell them anything,' said Hamish with a grin. He told her about the loan sharking.

'Good. We'll pull them in today and keep them in. No bail for them.' She took out a notebook and wrote in it and tore off a leaf. 'That's our address. Be there at seven this evening. I'll go and tell headquarters about the church. Get back there and pack up your stuff. If they're around, pick a quarrel with them and walk out.'

'Want coffee?' asked Hamish.

'No, I'll be off. See you later.'

Olivia made her way briskly out of the restaurant. It was then that Hamish realized he did not have enough money on him to pay the bill and that he had left his chequebook and bank cards back in Lochdubh, not wanting to take them to the church in case the Owens searched his belongings.

The dining room was empty apart from four other diners. Hamish's waitress appeared to be the only one on duty. She was standing looking out of the window.

'Here, you!' called Hamish rudely. 'What about bringing some coffee?'

She threw him an outraged look and stalked off into the kitchen.

Hamish slid out of his seat and was out of the restaurant and out of the hotel door as fast as he could.

He could not afford a cab and so had to walk all the way back to the church. To his relief, there was no sign of the Owens.

He packed up his few belongings and put them into Sean's old car and drove off.

He stopped at Sean's to pick up the police Land Rover and tried to persuade the old man to give him a refund because he hadn't had the car all week.

'Away with ye,' said Sean. 'That's a valuable car and twenty-five pounds was a damn cheap price for a week's rental. I should've charged you more.'

Hamish had a fleeting, treacherous thought that maybe he should have taken Tommy's parents' money.

He drove back to the police station.

Lochdubh lay spread out under a sunny, breezy sky. Wind whipped up the sea loch into waves. Washing on lines flapped gaily like flags welcoming him home. He felt he had been away for years instead of a matter of hours. Inside him, he felt a little twinge of dread. What if he could not pull it off? What if his cover was blown? What if it came to the crunch and he was asked for the money? He could not envisage Strathbane police head-quarters handing over fifty thousand pounds.

He let himself into the police station. He wished he could confide in someone, share the burden. But even if Priscilla should suddenly arrive back from London, he knew he could not even tell her.

He began to pack his one and only good suit and his few respectable shirts. He also packed several paperbacks. There might be long periods of waiting. He wondered about Olivia. Was she married? She must be tough and competent to have reached the rank of detect-ive inspector.

The police station was so comfortable, so familiar, so safe. It was tempting to manufacture some illness and beg off the job. With a sigh, he finished his packing, carried the suitcase out to the police Land Rover. He would drive it to headquarters, leave it there and walk along to his new address.

He drove to the doctor's and told Angela he was going to visit his parents in Rogart and stay with them for a bit. To his embarrassment, Angela made him wait while she took a cake out of the oven, let it cool and then boxed it up. 'It's lemon sponge,' said Angela. 'A present for your mother. Let me know how she likes it.'

Feeling guilty, Hamish took the cake and said his farewells.

Some time later, Olivia opened the door to him. Their 'new home' was a bungalow furnished in dreadful taste: fake log fire, velvet three-piece suite, noisy wallpaper, horrible oil paintings of hills and glens, glass coffee table and a giant television set.

'Who usually lives here?' asked Hamish, putting down his suitcase and placing the cake box on the coffee table.

'Some friend of Superintendent Peter Daviot who's letting us have the use of it. You brought cake?'

'Aye, one of my friends thought I was going to see my mother and gave me a cake for her.'

'We may as well have some. I'll make some tea. Your bedroom's second on the right down the corridor. Put your things away.'

She was wearing a shirt blouse tied at the waist and jeans. They should have put a man on the job, thought Hamish. It didn't matter how liberated the decade, women aroused protective feelings which could get in the way.

When he had put his things away, he returned to the living room. The sponge was on a plate with the tea things on the table.

'Your friend's sponge seems to have fallen in the middle,' said Olivia.

'Oh, well, that's Angela,' said Hamish. 'Heart of gold and the worst baking in the Highlands.'

'Maybe if we eat the outside and leave the soggy bit in the middle, it'll be all right.'

But it tasted as bad as it looked. Angela had used so much lemon and so little sugar that the sponge actually tasted sour.

'Don't let's bother with it,' said Olivia. 'Let's get down to business. You are a headman for Jimmy White's syndicate in Glasgow. You want to do business in the Highlands.'

'And what do the Highland lot think of that?'

'We'll find out. According to DC Sanders, who will be joining us shortly, they are a small outfit suddenly getting larger. Somehow, they are getting shipments of drugs into the country, undetected. Our job is to somehow find out where on the coast the supplies are coming in. Glasgow CID recently seized two shiploads so it's feasible that someone from Glasgow would come up here to purchase drugs.'

'Fifty thousand pounds is not going to impress them.'

'They're still not that large an outfit.' The doorbell rang. 'That'll be Sanders,' she said, going to answer it.

DC Sanders came in, looking more like a picture on a cornflakes packet than ever.

'Sit down, Sanders,' said Olivia. 'Tea?'

'Yes, milk and two sugars, please.'

'Help yourself,' said Olivia curtly, as if to say it was not a senior officer's job to pour tea just because that senior officer happened to be a woman.

'Tell Hamish what you know about the drug situation in Strathbane,' she commanded. 'I am getting in the way of calling him Hamish because we need to pose as man and wife.'

'It's like this,' said Sanders. 'We raided houses and arrested pushers. The pushers are usually small fry who are on drugs themselves. Through them we sometimes get one of the middlemen but never anyone at the top. Lachie's has been raided several times. We found some of the young people with ecstasy tablets but that was all.'

'What about Lachie's? Who owns it?'

'John Lachie. Up from Glasgow. Opened the disco a year ago,' said Sanders.

111

'Any record?'

'Early record. Robbery with violence. Did a stretch in Barlinnie Prison. That was ten years ago. Nothing since then.'

'What sort of man is he?' asked Hamish.

'Middle-aged, likes the high life, flashy car, flashy clothes. His disco's very popular. Young people come from all over the Highlands. There's not much else for them. If Lachie's the kingpin, then it's Lachie you'll meet tomorrow night. Could be someone else we don't know about.'

'What if Lachie gets on to Jimmy White?' asked Hamish uneasily. 'What if Jimmy White says he's neffer heard of me?'

'That's something we will deal with when the time comes,' said Olivia briskly. 'You will be issued with a gadget with an alarm button. You just press it and the place will immediately be flooded with police.'

'Meaning they will be on standby in the streets round about?'

'Yes,' said Sanders.

'I don't like it,' said Hamish.

'Why?' demanded Olivia.

'If they are dealing in hard drugs, they will be alert to any sign of police surveillance.'

'The men will be in plain clothes,' said Olivia testily.

'I can tell a Strathbane copper a mile off,' said Hamish, 'and I'm sure they can, too.'

112

Olivia looked at him impatiently. 'Then what do you suggest?'

'I suggest we take our chances. Headquarters isn't far from Lachie's. Why can't they wait there?'

'I'll see what I can do,' said Olivia uneasily, thinking of Superintendent Daviot's enthusiasm and of the maps he had pinned up on his office wall, of the fun he had had briefing the 'troops' personally. 'Wait here.'

She went off into her bedroom and then they could hear her voice as she spoke into her mobile phone.

'Grand cake,' said Sanders, eating busily.

'Have all you like,' said Hamish, thinking the man must have a cast-iron stomach.

'Quite a looker,' said Sanders.

'Olivia? She makes me uneasy,' said Hamish. 'They should have put a man on this job.'

'She's not a token woman appointment,' said Sanders. 'She's got a reputation of being clever and tough.'

'Is herself married?'

'No, and don't get any ideas. Some detective came on to her in Glasgow and she poured boiling coffee on him where it would hurt the most.'

'She is safe from me,' said Hamish. 'I tell you this, it is the long time since I've fancied any woman.'

'Wait till you see some of the nymphets at Lachie's.'

'I am not the baby-snatcher either.'

'Hamish Macbeth, I think you're a puritan.'

'How is he a puritan?' asked Olivia, coming into the room.

'He doesn't fancy the lassies.'

'Are you gay?' asked Olivia.

'No, I am not,' said Hamish. 'I am chust that wee bit disenchanted with women. What did headquarters say?'

'They're thinking about it. You know what the trouble is? There's just too many cop shows on television and Strathbane at the moment seems to be a case of life determined to imitate art. They swear no one will be able to detect their men.'

'Oh, aye,' remarked Hamish cynically. 'I'll bet they haff the street sweeper in sort of clean-dirty clothes out on the streets when every other street sweeper has packed it in for the day. Then there will be the ice cream van that doesn't sell ice cream. Oh, and what about the window cleaner cleaning windows in the dark? And the courting couple.'

'They're looking into it,' said Olivia curtly. 'We're going ahead with this because you got us into it in the first place. I hope you are not going to go on showing a lack of enthusiasm.'

'He's got a point, ma'am,' said Sanders uneasily.

'As I said, they are looking into it.'

'Well,' continued Sanders, 'what we are really looking for is a big shipment of heroin coming in. We've picked up whispers.'

'The monster,' said Hamish suddenly. 'The monster in Loch Drim.'

'What are you talking about?' demanded Olivia.

He told them about Ailsa thinking she had seen a monster. 'It could have been the light from a boat,' he said. 'Or they could have rigged up something to frighten the locals and keep them away.'

Olivia sat frowning in silence. Then she said, 'We're doing nothing this evening. We may as well drive over and have a look.'

'I'm on duty, ma'am,' said Sanders. 'Will I be expected to come with you?'

'No, that won't be necessary. We'll just have a recce.'

After Sanders had left, carrying the remains of the cake, Olivia made omelettes for them. After Hamish had washed up the dishes, she said, 'We'd better put on some dark clothes. You know the villagers there, don't you?'

'Yes, Drim is on my beat.'

'How will you explain me?'

'Monster fanatic. There's a lot of them around.'

They set out an hour later, Olivia driving. 'You know,' she said, 'I've never, ever been this far north in Scotland before.'

'No Highland holidays?'

'You know how it is, everyone goes abroad these days. Why spend a holiday in the Highlands of Scotland getting soaked to the skin when you can bask in the sunshine in Spain?'

'It's good for the complexion,' said Hamish. 'Just think of the damage the sun does to your skin.'

'And just think of the damage cold, wet weather does to your temper.'

'Aye, you could be right.'

'Tell me, Hamish, you seem to be an intelligent if unorthodox officer, and yet you're still only a policeman. Why is that?'

'I'm considered too much of a loose cannon for promotion. Besides, you've seen a wee bit of Strathbane. Would you like to work there?'

'It's not very different from Glasgow. Aren't you ambitious?'

'Not at all.'

'That's very odd.'

'I suppose it is, but it makes for a contented life. I love Lochdubh.'

'What's so special about the place?'

'It's easygoing, the people are friendly, I've got my bit of croft at the back of the police station. It's beautiful everywhere you look. If I moved to Strathbane, I'd be old before my time. I don't have to deal with any bad crime – well, not lately. The odd burglary, boundary disputes, sheep-dip papers, things like that.'

'Don't you get bored?'

'Hardly ever.'

'You're not married.'

'No,' said Hamish flatly.

'Which way now?'

'The signpost to Drim is just coming up. Make a left round the next bend.'

They made their way down the single-track winding road which led to Drim. Olivia could just make out the gleam of the sea loch. The wind had died down and everything was very still. A few lights twinkled in the cottages.

Because of the towering mountains above Drim and on either side of the loch, Olivia felt they were sinking down into complete blackness.

'Just stop the car outside the stores there,' said Hamish. 'We'll get out and walk.'

'I don't much like the atmosphere of this place,' said Olivia with a shiver. 'At least no one is about to see us.'

'Oh, they've seen us all right,' said Hamish. 'Every curtain in the village will have been twitching.'

'So why doesn't someone come out and ask us what we are doing?'

'That's not their way. They prefer to speculate. Much more fun. The path is along here. We'd better switch on our torches. As we get near the sea, we'll switch them off. The mountains fall back there, and there'll be enough light from the sky. I suggest we don't talk anymore. Sound carries a long way up here.'

He took out a black woollen hat and pulled it over his hair. 'Just in case we meet someone who shouldn't be here, my hair shines out like a beacon.'

After some time, they heard the sound of the sea and switched off their torches.

'All quiet,' whispered Olivia.

'Get down and don't make a sound,' Hamish hissed suddenly.

'What . . .?'

'I sense something.'

Hamish pulled up a clump of heather from the side of the path. 'Take some of the dirt and black your face.'

They smeared their faces and then waited in silence. Olivia began to relax. Hamish was a nice fellow but she was beginning to think he was eccentric, maybe a bit touched in the head.

She was just about to press his arm, to say something, when two great green eyes glared at them out of the blackness. 'Don't move,' urged Hamish. The eyes came closer. They were attached to a small head and long prehistoric neck. In the faint starlight, they could make out the coils of a serpentine body.

They waited. Olivia could feel cold sweat breaking out on her face. Then the creature turned and disappeared around the bend to the sea. Olivia tried to rise to her feet but

Hamish grabbed her shoulder and pulled her down. 'Wait!'

They waited for what seemed to Olivia like an age. Then Hamish rose and pulled her up and said, 'Come on. Let's see who's playing tricks.'

'We're unarmed and I don't have the thing with the panic button with me,' muttered Olivia. 'We're not in a position to confront drug smugglers.'

'I haff this feeling it is not the smugglers. Let's see.'

They walked quietly to the end of the loch. The sound of the sea was very loud now and would, Hamish hoped, drown any sounds of their approach.

'A cave. There must be a cave around here.'

His keen eyes scanned the steep rocks on either side of the entrance to the loch. 'Over there,' he whispered. 'Do you see that dark cleft? I bet it's there. Over on the other side.'

'How do we get over there?'

'We swim. You can swim?'

'Yes, but . . .'

'And you'd best keep close to me. The current can be strong.'

Olivia thought miserably as she entered the loch after Hamish that it must be the coldest water in the world. She was a strong swimmer but found she had to use every ounce of energy to battle with the current. Hamish reached down and pulled her up on the other side.

Together they approached the entrance to the cave. 'Just leave the thing to deflate,' said a voice. Jock Kennedy, thought Hamish. The bastard!

'Come on,' he said to Olivia. 'It isn't the drug smugglers.'

He strode into the cave. By the light of the hurricane lamp he saw Jock Kennedy and two men. The rubber neck of the monster was making a hissing sound as it deflated.

'Whit's the meaning of this, Jock?' demanded Hamish sternly.

'Och, it's yourself,' said Jock in a disgusted voice. 'I thought I had frightened you off.'

'What the hell were you up to?'

'Trade at the shop has been that slack. I thought if I had a monster and spread stories that the folks would come. You know what they're like in Drim, Hamish. They're aye putting the tourists off. I thought a monster would draw folks.'

'But you told me not to encourage Ailsa in thinking she had seen a monster.'

'Aye, but I didn't want *you* to take it seriously for I knew you would start poking your nose in.'

'How did you know we were on our way?'

Jock held up a mobile phone. 'We just happened to be along here putting more finishing touches.'

'Finishing is the word,' said Hamish bitterly. 'Get rid of that damn thing and, instead, try to

120

get the villagers to be nice to strangers. How did you get over here?'

'There's a track a bit up the mountain on this side.'

Olivia found her voice. 'Book him,' she said savagely.

'Oh, I don't think that will be necessary,' Hamish said soothingly. 'Jock won't be pulling that trick again.'

'Outside, Macbeth,' snapped Olivia.

He followed her out. 'You cannot be calling me Macbeth and giving me orders in front of the locals,' he chided, 'or they will guess you are a senior officer, and gossip spreads like wildfire in the Highlands. It wass only a prank and we've got more important work to do than charge Jock Kennedy. Surely the drug job is too important.'

'Just get me out of here,' she shouted.

Hamish went back into the cave. 'You'd best lead us back, Jock.'

'Who is the lady?'

'Some monster hunter like they get up in Loch Ness. And she's really sore with you.'

'Sorry,' mumbled Jock. 'But it was the grand monster.'

They silently followed him up the mountain and along a rocky track, broken in places by falls of scree.

Then they walked around the end of the loch to where Olivia's car was parked.

121

'Come in and dry yourselves and have a dram,' said Jock.

'That would be grand,' started Hamish, but Olivia said furiously, 'Just get in the car. We are leaving . . . *now*.'

'Very good,' said Hamish meekly.

Chapter Five

*What a lass that were to go a-gypseying
through the world with.*

– Charles Lamb

'Don't say anything at all,' she snapped as she drove towards Strathbane. 'I will speak to you when I am dry.'

When they arrived at the bungalow, Hamish followed her meekly in. 'I will use the bathroom first,' she said.

He went into the living room and switched on the electric heater and stood shivering in front of it.

At last she reappeared, dressed in a high-necked nightgown under a camel-hair man's dressing gown. 'Your turn,' she said.

He went off to the bathroom, stripped off, had a hot bath and, wrapping a large bath sheet about him, went to his bedroom and put on pyjamas and a dressing gown.

He went reluctantly back to the living room. 'Sit down, Macbeth,' she ordered.

He sat down.

'Now, let us go through that fiasco. First of all, you seemed to have forgotten I am your superior and gave me orders. You did not book those cheats either.'

'I had to tell you what to do,' said Hamish mildly, 'because I know the territory. There are things in the Highlands it iss better for a policeman to sort out without dragging people off to the courts. Think of the public expense of taking Jock to court and then it would come up who we are and what we were doing there and we cannae have that.'

'Is this an example of how you do your policing, Macbeth?'

He found himself becoming irritated with her, which in some part of his mind surprised him. He had been berated so many times by senior officers. Perhaps it was because of the very coldness and sexlessness of her manner.

'It iss in a way, ma'am. If a wee boy throws a ball and breaks a window, then the boy pays for new glass. If there's a boundary dispute and two crofters are threatening to go to the land court, I try to get them to sit down and talk and reach a compromise. If a woman had shoplifted something from Patel's, I haff a word with her. She usually doesn't do it again. If she does, and she is not poor and has a mental problem, kleptomania, I arrange with the doctor to have her sent to a psychiatrist. That way the state is saved a lot of expense, and some unfortunate people are saved from having a prison record. The benefit of being unambitious iss that I do not need notches on my belt. Also, tomorrow evening, while we are at Lachie's, I am supposed to be the big cheese and you are supposed to be my wife so I'll have to be in charge.'

She sat there, looking at him assessingly, the anger dying out of her eyes. At last she said, 'I should not be encouraging you to behave like a Wild West sheriff, but I suppose there is a mad Highland logic to your argument. Pour us both a nightcap and we will discuss tomorrow night.'

'What'll you have?' Hamish walked over to a trolley with an array of bottles.

'A malt.'

'Glenfiddich all right?'

'Fine.'

'What d'you want with it? Water? Soda?'

'Just straight.'

'I'll have the same.' Hamish poured two generous measures and handed one to her and sat down again.

'So,' she began, tucking her legs up under her and cradling her glass, 'what do you envisage will happen tomorrow?'

'I think Bob and Angus will get a rocket for being so loose-mouthed. I hope for their sakes that they're still alive. They'll have been grilled about how they took a complete stranger into their confidence. But whatever happens, they'll have to see me, if only to silence me permanently if they think I am an impostor. In order to get out of paying fifty thousand pounds, I will say that provided the quality of the stuff is good, then it's going to be a lot more than that. We've got to get friendly with them, socialize with them. The main point is to find out where the shipment comes in and when it is due. And I don't think we should continue to live here. I think we should check into the Grand.'

'Why?'

'This house belongs to some friend of Superintendent Daviot's. After they meet us, they'll check us out. A hotel is a more likely place for us to stay.'

She picked up a mobile phone from the side table next to her. 'I'll arrange that.'

'Wait a bit,' said Hamish, turning dark red with embarrassment. 'There's something else.'

She raised her eyebrows.

'After lunch yesterday, I found I hadn't enough money to pay the bill. So I ran away.'

'Didn't you have any cards on you?'

'I'd left my bank cards at Lochdubh, and, och, if we're checking in there, it's just as well I didn't use them. I mean, we won't be using our own names.'

'I don't know why everything you do seems to be a muddle. I'll get someone round to the hotel to pay for our lunch. Perhaps we should stay somewhere other than the Grand.'

'It's a lousy hotel, but it's the main one in Strathbane and fits the image we're trying to create.'

'Oh, very well. You can go to bed and leave me to sort this out.'

Hamish went off to bed, reflecting that even in her nightwear, Olivia managed to look every bit a chief inspector.

As he lay awake, he could hear the faint sound of her voice going on for what seemed like a long time. His thoughts returned to the Church of the Rising Sun. Why had Tommy gone to such a place? It had only been a brief meeting Hamish had had with the young man, and yet he had not got the impression of someone stupid. The Owens were into loan sharking. Could it not follow that they were into drugs as well? He lay awake wrestling with the problem. He should have told Olivia that the police should have been instructed to search for drugs.

He got out of bed and put on his dressing gown. The murmur of Olivia's voice on the phone had ceased. He went into the living room but it was in darkness. He knocked at the door of Olivia's bedroom. No reply.

He pushed open the door and went in.

By the moonlight streaming through the window and across the bed, he could see that she had fallen fast asleep.

He put a gentle hand on her shoulder and shook her.

She sat up in bed and let out a stifled scream. 'It's me – Hamish.'

'And just what the hell do you think you are doing in my bedroom, copper?' She switched on the bedside light. 'You are in deep shit, man. Making a pass at a senior officer.'

'*I am not making the pass at you,*' howled Hamish.

She looked up at him, the anger dying out of her eyes. He suddenly looked funny, standing there, his bright red hair ruffled, and a look of outrage on his face.

'Then why did you wake me up?'

'I couldn't sleep. I was thinking about them at the church, the Owens.' He told her about his theory that they might have been involved in drug dealing.

'I'll see to it,' she said wearily. 'But you'd better pray they don't find anything.'

'Why?'

'Because if the Owens were into supplying drugs to their parishioners, then it follows that one of the congregation might be found at Lachie's and recognize you.'

'Then let's hope I'm wrong,' said Hamish.

'Go back to bed,' she said. 'I'll deal with it.'

Hamish awoke in the morning with the beginnings of fear in his stomach. The fear was not that he would be exposed as a fraud and so put his life in danger. The fear was that he would not be able to carry it off and lose face with Olivia. He had to admit he found her attractive, very attractive. He was irked that she regarded him in a totally sexless light.

When he went into the kitchen, she was reading the newspapers. 'We'll be moving to the Grand after you cook us some breakfast,' she said when she saw him. 'That's our car outside. I think we should get into the part right away.'

'Very well, darling.'

'*What* did you call me?'

'Chust getting into the act of being your husband,' said Hamish.

'Well, don't unless there is anyone else around. There's a suitcase of clothes arrived for you as well.'

'I haff the verra good suit,' said Hamish huffily.

'Probably too conservative for the part you're supposed to play.'

'I'll have a look.'

'Breakfast first, if you please. I'll have coffee and two poached eggs on toast.'

I find you attractive but I could really learn to dislike you, thought Hamish.

After he had cooked and they had eaten breakfast, he looked out of the front window of the bungalow. A gleaming gold Mercedes was parked outside.

'Where did they get the car from?' he asked.

'Up from Glasgow. I don't know where they got it from. We'd best go and get changed and get out of here.'

Hamish picked up the suitcase and went into his bedroom, slung it on the bed and opened it. There was an Armani suit, designer jeans, suede and leather jackets, silk underwear, shirts with the name of a famous Jermyn Street shirt maker and a box containing gold cuff links, gold Rolex and wraparound sunglasses. There was also a camel-hair coat.

There was a wallet containing credit cards in the name of Hamish George, a passport and driving licence. It was odd, he thought, when one was at the very bottom of the police force rung, how one would never dream that they could get all this stuff ready so quickly.

He wished he could wear his own clothes. But when he was finally dressed in the biscuit-coloured Armani suit, shirt, silk tie, gold cuff links and gold watch, he realized what a good idea it was. He felt like an actor dressed for a part.

Carrying the coat over his arm, he went into the living room and sat down to wait for Olivia. At last her bedroom door opened and she came out. Hamish blinked at the transformation.

There was now something subtly common and coarse about Olivia. Her hair was piled on top of her head in an elaborate arrangement of curls and loops. She was wearing a power-dressing suit, large shoulder pads, very short skirt and with the jacket worn over a white silk blouse decorated with many gold chains. She wore heavy eye make-up and had painted her mouth to look much fuller and pouting. Her stiletto heels had platform soles.

She pirouetted in front of him. 'Well, do I look like a drug dealer's wife?'

'I don't know what one looks like,' said Hamish, 'but I should think she'd look like you.'

'Right, let's get all our stuff into the car. I have good news for you. They have given us a couple of bodyguards.'

'Why?'

'Because that will add to our image. It also gives us protection. They'll be waiting for us at the hotel.'

Hamish found he was slightly irritated that they were not to be on their own. He was afraid that their 'muscle' might turn out to be two plainclothes who positively shouted out that they were detectives.

Once their new belongings were loaded in – Olivia had said to leave their own stuff behind and someone would pick it up later – he drove the Mercedes towards the Grand Hotel.

He passed over one of his credit cards, startled at the price of the room, which seemed to him a horrendous amount. But then the Grand was a pretentious hotel.

It turned out that a suite had been booked for them. There was a sitting room with bar and television, a large bedroom with a double bed and en suite bathroom and then a small bedroom off it. Olivia indicated the small bedroom. 'That's where you will be sleeping.'

'Don't you think the hotel staff will find it odd that a powerful man like me doesn't sleep with his wife?' asked Hamish.

She looked at him with a frown. 'Damn, I suppose you're right. Just keep to your own side of the bed.'

'Yes, ma'am.'

'And you'd better get used to calling me Olivia.'

The phone rang and Olivia jumped a little. So she had nerves after all. She answered it and said, 'Come along.'

She turned to Hamish. 'That's our muscle. Let's have a look at them.'

After a few moments, there was a knock at the door. Two huge men walked in. It was in that moment that Hamish realized that a lot of detectives, apart from the fresh-faced Sanders, actually looked like hoods. All you had to do was change the clothes. Both men were wearing conservative suits, but one had a black shirt and no tie and the other a scarlet shirt, also no tie. They had the stone-dead eyes of hardened criminals.

They sat down and surveyed each other. 'You're not from Glasgow,' said Olivia.

'No, Scotland Yard. Drug squad,' said one with a face like a hatchet. 'I am DC Brompton and this is DC King.'

'I'll need your first names.'

'Kevin and Barry.'

'Right. Now I, as you have probably been briefed, am Chief Inspector Chater. You will from now on call me Mrs George. This is PC Hamish Macbeth, who is posing as my husband, Hamish George. We'll now go over everything again.'

As she outlined how Hamish had got them into all this, their new bodyguards listened stolidly. But occasionally one of them would flick a deadpan look in Hamish's direction and Hamish could sense each of them was silently damning him as some amateur Highland fool.

Olivia summed up. 'So the meet is tonight at Lachie's at nine o'clock. We'll take it from there.'

Hamish was becoming increasingly worried. A lot of money had already been laid out on this operation. What if, so his anxious thoughts ran, Angus and Bob were nothing more than drug *takers* and would introduce him to some friend at Lachie's posing as a drug baron so that they could pick up their fee?

Kevin spoke. 'I don't like the idea of Hamish posing as an associate of Jimmy White. In the underworld of drugs, gossip travels fast. You don't want Jimmy saying he's never even heard of him. I would suggest, make Hamish

133

the head of a new syndicate with ties to Turkey. If the money he's offering seems to be big enough, then they might take the bait.'

The three of them discussed this idea as if Hamish wasn't there.

At last Hamish felt he ought to assert himself. 'Why don't you just let me play it by ear?' he said.

'Are you good at that?' asked Barry doubtfully.

'Och, yes,' said Hamish with a confidence he did not feel.

'I think that's all we can do now,' said Olivia briskly. 'Lachie's is quite close. We'll leave here at ten to nine.'

After the bodyguards had left, Olivia dialled police headquarters on her mobile to ask if they had raided the Owens place yet and if anything had been found. She listened carefully and then rang off. 'They're going through the Owens home and the church at the moment. We'll need to wait a bit.'

Hamish took out one of his paperbacks and started to read. Olivia paced up and down.

'I don't know how you can be so calm!' she burst out.

'The way I see it,' said Hamish, putting his book down, 'is that if we can't do anything right now, we may as well find ways to pass the time.'

'I suppose,' she said restlessly.

'I tell you what,' said Hamish. 'We take that monster of a car out for a drive. It's a grand day. May as well show you the scenery.'

Soon they were driving away from Strathbane. 'I've never had a car like this afore,' said Hamish. 'Look at all these gadgets.'

'Where are we going?'

'I thought I might show you Lochdubh.'

'You'll be recognized.'

'I've an idea.' Hamish swung the car around. He drove back a little way into town and stopped outside a shop. He went in and emerged with a down-the-river hat, which after he had got in the car, he put on. Then he took the wraparound sunglasses out of his pocket and put them on as well. 'No one in Lochdubh will recognize me like this,' he said.

He drove off again. 'When we get to Lochdubh I'd like to take you for a walk about the place but that would be too risky.'

'The scenery's incredible,' said Olivia. 'So wild, so savage.'

'Sometimes in winter it can be very bleak,' said Hamish, 'but the landscape is never the same. The changing light alters the perspective so that the mountains never look the same.'

'So much purple heather,' murmured Olivia.

'You'll have the heather on the mountains at Loch Lomond.'

'But not like this! Miles and miles of purple flowers. And that yellow gorse. So much colour.'

The big car cruised towards Lochdubh. 'I must admit,' said Hamish, 'there are a lot of moments when I wish I had minded my own business. I wish right now I were going home, back to the police station.'

Olivia looked at him curiously. 'You really love it here, don't you?'

'Yes, I'm happy most of the time,' said Hamish, 'except when I land myself in things like this.'

Detective Chief Inspector Blair called in early at police headquarters. Superintendent Peter Daviot espied him and summoned him to his office. 'I thought you weren't due back until Monday,' said Daviot.

'Oh, you know me,' said Blair with a cheesy smile. 'Can't keep me away from the office.'

'We have a big secret operation going on here,' said Daviot, and told him about Hamish Macbeth posing as a drug baron.

Blair listened intently. From Daviot's enthusiasm for what he privately thought was a daft scheme, he knew that any rubbishing of Hamish Macbeth would not go down well.

'And what would you like me to do, sir?' he asked when Daviot had finished.

'There's nothing you can do at the moment,'

said Daviot. 'May as well enjoy the few days off you have left.'

Blair went thoughtfully out of police head-quarters. He walked to the nearest pub, head down like a charging bull. Once inside, he ordered a double whisky, downed it in one and ordered another. He was in a flaming temper. That Hamish Macbeth should be getting all this glory was almost beyond bearing.

After another double whisky, he began to dream about a scenario in which the drug dealers were tipped off that Hamish was an undercover cop. The silly Highland loon would end up floating face-downward in the docks. After yet another whisky, he began to wonder if he should tip someone off. That way he would be rid of Hamish Macbeth – permanently.

'And this is Lochdubh,' said Hamish proudly, stopping the car on the top of the hill.

'They should have signs in the Highlands with phonetic spelling under the place names,' said Olivia. 'I mean do most people know it's pronounced Lochdoo? And what does it mean?'

'Black loch,' said Hamish. 'Well, what do you think of the place?'

The village of Lochdubh was situated in a gentle curve along the loch below two towering mountains. The lines of eighteenth-century whitewashed cottages with their flower-filled gardens and flapping washing on the lines basked in the sun. A light breeze rippled the surface of the loch. Across the loch lay an expanse of forestry and through the open car window Olivia could smell pine.

'It looks very pretty,' she commented. 'What's that big building down by the harbour? A private house?'

'It used to be a hotel,' said Hamish. 'It's still up for sale.'

'I'm surprised there are no takers. It's a lovely site.'

'I hope someone buys it soon,' said Hamish. 'It would be a pity if a grand building like that should fall into a ruin.'

He drove on, over the humpbacked bridge which spanned the River Anstey.

'Could you envisage living in a place like this?' he asked.

Olivia laughed. 'In my dreams. In reality, I would probably die of boredom. Don't you ever get bored?'

'Not in Lochdubh,' said Hamish.

'So what do you do?'

'I have a bit of a croft – there, you can just see it behind the police station. I'll circle round by the harbour and then we'll get out of here just in case I am recognized.'

Olivia was to remember that afternoon as the calm before the storm as they drove slowly along country roads, stopping for lunch at a small pub, then driving on again until Hamish said reluctantly, 'Time to go back. The light is failing.'

'Why aren't you married?' asked Olivia.

'The right girl, the wrong time, the wrong place, that sort of thing. What about you?'

'I'm married to my job.'

'No yearning for romance, a home, children?'

'No,' she said curtly.

They drove the rest of the way towards Strathbane in silence. The companionship that had grown up between them on the drive had evaporated.

When they got back to the hotel room, Hamish asked, 'Should we have dinner before we go?'

'I feel too strung up to eat anything. Why don't we just order a sandwich from room service?'

'Anything in particular?'

'Ham and salad.'

Hamish picked up the phone and ordered the sandwiches and a pot of coffee. Olivia had switched on the television and was watching the news.

Then her mobile phone rang, making them both jump. She listened intently. Then Olivia said, 'That's a much more sensible idea. I never liked Macbeth's plan in the first place. Too risky. I think they'll go for this.' She listened some more and then rang off.

'The new plan is this,' she said briskly. 'We

could be in trouble if they think you're some new drug dealer muscling in on their territory. Before I tell you what it is, they did not find any drugs at the Owens place. Now, here is what you are supposed to be. You have a shipment of heroin, prime stuff, all the way from the East and through Amsterdam. Originally out of the Highlands, you nonetheless operate mostly from Istanbul. You mostly sell to France, Spain and Belgium, but now you want to expand and sell some here. But where do you land it? That's what you want to get out of them. Glasgow still has that load of drugs they seized. We can use that as bait. Once they take the bait and say they'll buy, then they'll tell us where and when, and we'll have them. Offer them four kilos of heroin to start with.'

'And how much is that?' asked Hamish. 'I mean, it can be as much as a hundred pounds per gram on the streets, but a dealer is going to pay less for the raw stuff.'

'You'll be selling it at twenty thousand a kilo.'

'This means entrapment?' said Hamish. 'I don't like it. I'd rather have caught them with their own stuff and get some of that off the market.'

'You'll do as you're told,' said Olivia sharply.

An actor must feel like this just before going on stage, thought Hamish as he and Olivia with Kevin and Barry close behind walked into Lachie's disco at nine that evening.

The place was full of gyrating couples. The music pounded and beat upon the smoky air and strobe lights stabbed down from the ceiling.

They made their way to the long bar which ran along the far side of the room.

Hamish wondered, before making his order, whether a drug baron would order something showy with an umbrella stuck in it, but Olivia asked for a whisky so he ordered two.

Olivia was wearing a slinky flame-coloured dress with thin shoulder straps and carrying a black cashmere shawl over one arm. Her dress was more like a petticoat than a dress, thought Hamish. It was even edged with flame-coloured lace at the short hemline.

Her hair was worn loose on her shoulders. Her scarlet lips, which had been painted to look fuller and more pouting, gave her a vulgar, sultry look. 'What a place,' she shouted to Hamish above the din, and then gave a loud, empty raucous laugh. May as well get into the part as well, thought Hamish. He put an arm about Olivia's shoulders and, bending down, kissed her on the mouth. Olivia gazed up at him adoringly and said in a low voice, 'Don't do that again.'

'Just acting,' said Hamish. His eyes scanned the room. He could see no sign of either Bob or Angus. His heart began to sink. He had caused this highly expensive operation on the word of a couple of layabouts who probably did not know anyone in the drug trade.

Ten minutes passed. 'If they were serious,' said Kevin, 'they'd have been here on time.'

'I knew there was something stupid about this whole thing,' said Olivia, not bothering to lower her voice.

Hamish scanned the room. The music thudded, the strobe lights flashed, couples gyrated round each other as if performing some ritual tribal dance.

And then he glimpsed Bob. He appeared to be searching.

It was then that Hamish realized that despite his red hair, Bob probably wouldn't recognize him in his Armani suit, camel coat draped about his shoulders and wraparound sunglasses.

Hamish said to Barry and Kevin, 'There's a fat, little fellow looking for me. I'll try to point him out to you and then I think you should both fetch him over.'

His eyes raked over the dancers. 'There!' he said. 'Chust to the left. The one with the snake tattooed around his arm.'

Kevin and Barry moved forward. Hamish saw them speaking to Bob. As Bob was led forward, he did not look nearly so pugnacious. He gave Hamish a sort of smirk. 'Didnae recognize you,' he said.

'Am I wasting my time?' asked Hamish.

'No, no,' grovelled Bob, although his eyes devoured Olivia's cleavage. 'I'll be right back.'

He disappeared into the swirl of dancers. 'Things are moving,' hissed Olivia.

After a few minutes, a tall, thin lugubrious man like an undertaker materialized in front of them. He was even wearing a black suit and black tie.

'Come with me,' he said.

They followed him to a door next to the far end of the bar. He opened the door and ushered them into an office. 'Just call me Lachie,' said the man behind the desk, getting to his feet. He was middle-aged, going thin on top, fat creased babyish face, little rosebud mouth, expensively cut dark suit but worn over a shirt embroidered with silver bells. No tie.

Behind him stood two goons, a sort of mirror image of Kevin and Barry.

A small dapper man with a lot of gold jewellery lounged in an armchair in a shadowy corner of the room.

Hamish suddenly sensed Olivia's acute nervousness and wondered why. Olivia, unknown to Hamish, had recognized the man in the corner of the room as Jimmy White from Glasgow. She was beginning to fear Hamish would not be able to pull off this scam.

'Sit down,' said Lachie expansively. 'Drink?'

'No,' said Hamish, swinging his coat off his shoulders and handing it to Kevin. 'You've kept me waiting and I want to get down to business.'

'That idiot Bob spent too long looking for you,' said Lachie. 'You could have chosen a brighter contact. Who put you on to Bob?'

Hamish sat down and leaned back in his chair. 'Mind your own business,' he said insolently.

'So what's your business?' demanded Lachie. 'Interested in buying?'

'No, I only said that for the sake of the idiot Bob. I'm selling.'

'Oh, aye. Selling what?'

'Shipment of heroin.'

'How much?'

'Four kilos for starters.'

'Four . . . where have you got this stuff?'

The little man in the corner spoke for the first time. 'I think you should all get out o' here and let me have a word wi' . . .?'

'George. Hamish George.'

'We stay,' said Kevin.

Lachie looked at Jimmy. The two goons behind him crowded in closer to the desk.

'Why not?' said Hamish easily. 'Look after my beautiful wife.'

Kevin and Barry instinctively looked to Olivia for guidance. She stood up, draping her cashmere stole over her arm. 'Oh, come along. I need a drink,' she pouted. She leaned over Hamish and kissed him full on the mouth, and then said, 'It's Jimmy White,' in a breath of a voice.

They all went out and Jimmy White moved round and sat behind the desk.

Apart from his gold identity bracelet, gold watch and thick gold chain around his neck, Jimmy White could pass for an ordinary Scottish businessman, thought Hamish, if it were not for the stone-hard look of his small black eyes.

'I'm Jimmy White,' he said. 'This is all a bit sudden, as the actress said to the bishop. Nobody's ever heard of you and you stroll in here with this damn offer.'

'I work out of Istanbul,' said Hamish. He suddenly remembered a name he had heard when one of his investigations had taken him to London and he had overheard some detectives in Scotland Yard gossiping. 'Heard of Cherokee Jim?'

'Aye. But he's cocaine.''

'And I'm heroin. This is beginning to sound a bit like "me Tarzan, you Jane". Are you interested or not?'

'Maybe. Why come up here?'

'Because I was born here. I need someplace safe to land the stuff. I haven't been back here since I was a boy so I don't know the places that will escape the investigations of Customs and Excise.'

'How did you get started?'

Hamish stared at him for a long moment. 'I don't see why the fuck I should waste time answering stupid questions about my background.' Hamish, who hardly ever swore, hoped he wasn't blushing. 'You either want the stuff or you don't.'

'Oh, I want it. Those bastards in Glasgow seized a haul. Look, mac, how can I trust you?'

'You can't. You have to take my word for it, tell me where to land it, come with me, bring as much muscle as you like.' Hamish stifled a yawn.

'You're a cool bugger. When Lachie told me that idiot Bob had been blabbing to someone he knew nothing about, I could have killed him. But I'll tell you one thing you're not. You're not an undercover cop. When I heard from Lachie, I was sure you were.'

'And what would you have done? Killed me?'

'You know we don't go around killing coppers unless they're bent,' sneered Jimmy. 'The minute I clapped eyes on you and that wife of yours, I knew I was looking at one of my own kind. You know what's kept me on top? Brains.'

'Well, we can sit here all night talking about your brilliance,' said Hamish, 'or we can get down to business. Do we have a deal?'

'Yes, but you'll need to wait a week. How much are you asking?'

'Twenty thousand a kilo.'

146

'Right. Where are you staying?'

'The Grand. Why a week?'

'I'll need to discuss this with my associates. You know how it is.'

'Okay. But don't make it any longer.'

'It's funny, mind,' said Jimmy, 'that I haven't heard of you.'

'I usually keep in the background. Only fools get themselves too well known.'

'Right. What about some dinner?'

'Had it, thanks,' said Hamish, who had no wish to prolong the agony of his act a moment longer than necessary.

'When I get back, then. Your wife's a real smasher. Funny, I've got a feeling I've seen her somewhere before. Was she on the films?'

'She doesn't do that any more and she knows I'd cut her face if she did,' said Hamish harshly.

'Oh, *those* sort of films.'

'Aye, but we will not be talking about that.'

'Sure, sure.'

Hamish stood up and slung his coat around his shoulders. He put on his dark glasses.

'See you,' he said laconically, and strolled out, resisting a strong impulse to run.

A flicker of relief darted through Olivia's eyes when she saw him.

Hamish put an arm around her shoulders. 'Come on, babe, let's get out of here.'

* * *

Back in the hotel room, Hamish told them about how he had got on. He finished by saying, 'He thought he had seen you somewhere before, Olivia. Is that possible?'

'When I was made chief inspector,' said Olivia, 'my photo was in the Glasgow papers.'

'You should have told me that,' said Hamish impatiently. 'Anyway, I managed to convince him that he had seen you in a blue movie.'

Kevin gave a great laugh. 'The first time I heard of anyone looking at their faces.'

'Show a bit of respect,' snapped Olivia. 'What do we do for a week?'

'We wait,' said Hamish. 'Lounge about. Spend the state's money.'

'Won't do. They'll be watching us and they'll probably search the hotel room. Wait a minute. I've a phone call to make.'

She picked up the mobile and went into the bedroom.

'That's one for the book,' said Barry. 'Imagine anyone thinking old concrete knickers had been in a blue movie. You have the fair gift o' the gab, Hamish.'

Hamish found he was about to protest strongly at anyone calling Olivia concrete knickers but decided against it. She was only a pretend wife and he had heard senior male officers dubbed with much ruder names.

'I think we could all do with a drink,' said Kevin. 'What's your poison, Hamish?' He opened the minibar.

'I'll stick to whisky.'

The two detectives had beer.

'So what's a bright lad like you doing as a village copper?' asked Barry when they were seated around with their drinks.

Hamish sighed. 'I'm sick o' explaining. I like the job, I like Lochdubh.'

'But where's the life, the excitement?' asked Kevin.

'I've found happiness has got little to do with thrills and spills,' said Hamish patiently.

'Oh, you'll grow up one day if it's not too late and get into the real world.'

'And one day you'll find you're the children and I'm the grown-up,' said Hamish. 'Oh, shut up about it. I'm tired.'

'You must have done a grand job,' said Kevin. 'Jimmy White's the worst of criminals. He's got brains.'

Hamish took a sip of whisky. 'Not as much as he thinks he has and that's his weakness.'

Olivia came in. She had changed into trousers and a shirt blouse and had scrubbed her face clean of make-up. Her hair was pulled back into a severe knot. Both detectives, who had been lounging in their chairs, straightened up.

'This is what we have decided,' said Olivia briskly. 'If we hang around here for a week, we will be followed. They'll be checking up on us. So tomorrow, we are going to Amsterdam. That is supposed to be your last port of operation outside the UK, Hamish, so that's where we'll go. Someone will contact us while we are there.' She looked at Kevin and Barry. 'There will be no need for you to join us. I do not think we will be in any danger until the action starts.'

'Do we drive there?' asked Hamish.

'No, we leave the car at Inverness Airport, fly down to London and catch a plane from there. They will send round our tickets and money in the morning.'

'I hope nobody around at police headquarters is gossiping,' said Hamish anxiously.

'Only a few of the top brass are in the know,' said Olivia. 'Surely you trust your senior officers, Hamish.'

The answer to that one was no, not at all. But Hamish did not think it would be politic to say so.

'So the jammy bastard's got hisself a trip tae Amsterdam,' growled Blair over a glass of whisky as he looked across the bar room table at Jimmy Anderson.

'Aye, and he's pretending to be husband to that chief inspector from Glasgow and she's a looker by all accounts.'

Jealousy like bile rose up in Blair's throat. If only he could get rid of Hamish Macbeth for once and for all.

Chapter Six

'Twas for the good of my country that I should be abroad – Anything for the good of one's country.

– George Farquhar

Hamish sat on a British Airways flight to Amsterdam and wished he could thaw the atmosphere between himself and Olivia.

They had shared the hotel bed the night before, each lying chastely as far away from the other as possible. But somehow during the night he had, in his sleep, put an arm around her and gathered her close and Olivia had awoken first to find her head pillowed on his chest and herself held fast in his embrace.

She had woken him, demanded to know what the hell he was about, taking advantage of the situation. In vain he had protested that it must have happened in his sleep.

They had been tailed by the man Hamish had dubbed the Undertaker to Inverness Airport but as far as he knew they were no longer being followed. Of course, the Undertaker could have found out they were on the plane and a tail could pick them up in Amsterdam.

So here he was bound for his first foreign trip with a pretty woman who was just about as much company as Chief Inspector Blair would have been.

Hamish thought of the now silly dreams he had nourished while falling asleep beside her, how they would walk along the canals, see the museums, and just perhaps, just perhaps, something might happen between them.

The plane began its descent to Schiphol Airport. 'Where are we staying?' asked Hamish, breaking the heavy silence.

'The Hilton.'

More silence. Hamish sighed. Come into the twentieth century, he chided himself. If she were a man and your senior officer, you would be quiet and respectful. She must be used to men coming on to her.

Hamish nonetheless could not help feeling excited as the taxi bore them the eighteen kilometres into Amsterdam. He was abroad. If only he had a camera, so that when this was all over, he could show the folks in Lochdubh that he, Hamish Macbeth, had actually been abroad. Of course, he could probably buy one of those disposable ones. He could see Anne Frank's house, take a trip by boat along the canals, buy some souvenirs. He must buy a present for Angela.

They arrived at the Hilton, which over-looked the Amstel. He was relieved to see their room had twin beds.

'Did you notice if we were followed from the airport?' asked Olivia briskly.

'No, ma'am. But they might send someone over.'

Hamish unpacked his suitcase and then looked hopefully out of the window. There were lights glittering along the canal.

'Would you care to go for a walk before dinner?' he asked.

'No, we will wait. We are to be contacted.'

Hamish sighed, picked up a paperback and slumped down in an armchair by the window.

He would have liked a cup of coffee, but Olivia was exuding such a terrifying air of chilly authority that somehow he did not dare, and he resented her at the same time. Damn all women. Why couldn't he forget she was a woman?

The phone rang. She answered it, listened and said, 'Send him up.'

Hamish looked up at her inquiringly, but obviously he was still in the doghouse and expected to wait until she chose to tell him.

He stifled another sigh. Here he was in this exciting city with a pretty woman and he was trapped in this hotel room, rather as if he was some foreign dignitary under house arrest.

There was a knock at the door. Olivia opened it. A small dapper man entered. He was balding, had a round smooth face and gold-rimmed glasses.

'I am Pieter Willet,' he said, holding out a plump, well-manicured hand. He looked at Hamish, who had got to his feet. 'And you are this British chief inspector?'

'I am Chief Inspector Chater,' said Olivia frostily. 'This is Police Constable Hamish Macbeth.'

Pieter bent over her hand and deposited a kiss somewhere in the air above it. 'Apologies, dear lady. I did not expect such beauty.'

Olivia gave him a nasty sort of cut-the-bullshit look, but said, 'And you are? I mean your job?'

'I am attached to the drug squad but always undercover. I am a good person to send to you because my face is never connected to that of the police. Were you followed?'

'Not that we know of. But we feel sure there will be someone in Amsterdam shortly.'

'We will go out for dinner and let them find us. We will discuss our plans over dinner. You are my guests.'

'That's verra kind of you,' said Hamish with a charming smile.

Oh, that frosty look of Olivia's! Wasn't he even supposed to be civil?

'Do we have to change for dinner?' she asked.

Pieter surveyed her rather tight suit, very

short skirt and low-cut blouse. 'You look delightful as you are.'

'I do not normally dress like this,' said Olivia. 'But as I am supposed to be his wife –' she jerked a thumb at Hamish – 'I may as well look the part.'

'Some of the top drug barons favour a French restaurant called Moulin Rouge. You may as well start to look part of the underworld scene.'

'Will I have to talk to any of them?' asked Hamish. He caught Olivia's cold look and said impatiently, 'Look, ma'am, the minute we go out, you are my wife and I'm the one who has to do the talking.'

'Some may approach our table. I am known as a businessman, importer-exporter. You will not need to do any business. You're an associate of mine, that's all. But if anyone is watching, then it will create the right effect. Shall we go?'

As tall buildings, canals, bridges glittering with lights, and gaily painted boats flew past, Hamish longed to be able to get out and walk around. He felt quite sulky, rather like a child being taken to the seaside and told to stay indoors and do his homework. He didn't want to go to some French restaurant favoured by villains. He wanted to try Dutch cooking. He wanted to shop for souvenirs and take photographs. He began to wonder if he could give Olivia the slip the following day.

He was sitting in the back, Olivia in the front with Pieter, who was driving. Hamish looked out of the back window. There was a black BMW behind. He could not make out who was driving it. He waited a few minutes until Pieter had made a right-hand turn down a narrow street. There was now a little red car behind, two cyclists and, behind that, turning slowly into the street, the black BMW.

He kept glancing back. The BMW was always there, sometimes close behind them, sometimes letting two cars get between them.

On they went, now in a broad thoroughfare, past clanking trams, then another right-hand turn and along a side street, and finally in front of them in a square was the Moulin Rouge, not, despite its name, in an old windmill like some of the famous Amsterdam restaurants like De Molen De Dikkert, but a low modern building with a fake neon-illuminated windmill on its roof.

'There's parking round the back,' said Pieter.

Hamish looked round as the car drove into the car park at the back of the restaurant. No BMW.

They all got out and began to walk towards the front of the restaurant. Pieter and Olivia, arm in arm, walked ahead of Hamish into the restaurant. Despite its garish outside, inside was expensively quiet and smooth, expanses of white linen, mahogany and brass and the smells of good cooking.

'I'll be with you in a minute,' Hamish called to the retreating backs of Pieter and Olivia, who were following the maître d' to a table in the far corner.

He went out of the restaurant and looked around. Then he walked quickly around to the car park. He stood in the shadows at the entrance. The black BMW was just being parked. Then the man Hamish called the Undertaker got out. Two other men also got out. The Undertaker said something to them and then got in behind the wheel. The two men began to walk out of the car park. One was small and swarthy, wearing a blazer with some improbable crest on the pocket and flannels with turn-ups and suede shoes. The other was taller, wearing a black leather jacket over jeans. He was bald, with a tired crumpled face.

'You'd better put a tie on, Sammy,' said his companion. Glaswegians, thought Hamish. Jimmy White's men. He walked swiftly back to the restaurant.

He joined Olivia and Pieter. 'They've caught up with us. Two of them are about to walk into the restaurant. And Olivia, *dear*, chust a wee point. You may be flaming mad with me but as you're supposed to be my wife, you don't walk ahead of me into a restaurant with another man. Here they come.'

Olivia looked at them covertly over the top of a large leather-bound menu. 'Look like a couple of idiots,' she said. 'Nonetheless, they have to report back. Is there any hope that your villainous friends will be here tonight?'

'Oh, I should think so,' said Pieter. 'Let's order.'

'Is the food any good?' asked Hamish.

'What there is of it,' said Pieter dryly.

It turned out to be nouvelle cuisine, that genre of cooking which saves any restaurateur great expense. Hamish, for the main course, had ordered pigeon. He looked gloomily down at two pigeon drumsticks on a bed of rocket, one small potato and one tomato cut to look like a flower.

'I would never have thought,' he said to Pieter, 'that the top honchos of the drug world would have dined in a place like this. I would have thought decent platefuls of food would have been more in their line.'

'They feel safe with the proprietor.'

'Oh, is that it? I'll need to order some sandwiches when I get back to the hotel.'

'Ah, here's the American contingent.'

'I'll need to change my ideas about what a drug baron's wife should wear,' said Olivia, studying the newcomers. Two men, who looked exactly like wealthy American businessmen, were sitting down at a table in the centre with two women. One woman was a statuesque blonde in a slinky dress and very high heels. She had a beautiful face and her make-up was perfect. The other woman was middle-aged, in a smart silk trouser suit, her iron-grey hair carefully styled. Olivia looked ruefully down at her own plunging blouse and push-up bra. 'Trust the powers that be to think I had to dress like a tart. Will they come over?'

'They'll probably drop by the table to exchange a few words. They're well known in the drug world, so your minders will have something to talk about. It looks like a quiet night, so you're lucky they've turned up.'

Hamish looked in amusement at the two Glaswegians, who were staring at the tiny portions on their plates as if they couldn't believe their eyes.

They were just finishing their coffee when one of the Americans approached their table. He was a large man with a gin-and-sauna face.

'Evening, Pieter,' he said.

'Evening, Gus. Let me introduce you. This is Hamish George, a Scottish businessman, and his wife, Olivia. Hamish, Olivia, Gus Peck.'

Gus drew up a chair and sat down. 'And what's your line of business, Hamish?' he asked.

'Same as Pieter's,' said Hamish. 'Import-export.'

'How about that?' said Gus, clapping him on the shoulder. 'I'm in the same line of business myself. Where are you staying?'

'The Hilton.'

'Vacation?'

'Business and pleasure.'

'Hope to see you around. Pieter knows where to find me.'

He rose and smiled expansively and went back to his table.

'I hope that does some good,' said Hamish. 'But will our minders know who he is?'

'They'll probably get his name from the maître d' and phone it to Jimmy White and Jimmy White will recognize the name. Gus is big.'

'If you know all these villains, it stands to reason the police know who they are,' said Hamish. 'So why don't they pick them up?'

Pieter shrugged. 'All these sort of men have impeccable cover. I just keep my ear to the ground and tip the police off from time to time if I get word of any shipments of drugs, but not too often. I have my own cover to maintain.'

Olivia stifled a yawn. 'Let's go. I'm tired. What's on the cards for tomorrow?'

'I'll take you to a nightclub tomorrow evening where they all hang out,' said Pieter. 'We don't really need to do anything during your week. Just be seen in all the right places.'

'Our minders don't seem to be following,' said Olivia as they left the restaurant.

'It's more important to them to stay behind,' said Hamish, 'and find out Gus's identity. Besides, they know where we're staying.'

* * *

Later that evening Hamish and Olivia lay in their twin beds. There was still a distinct frost emanating from Olivia. She was reading a magazine.

'Olivia,' ventured Hamish.

'What?'

'As we're not to be doing anything until tomorrow evening, we could spend the day looking around, visit some of the sights.'

'We will stay here,' said Olivia crossly. 'Have you forgotten you're supposed to know Amsterdam? Not ponce about like some bloody tourist.'

I hate her, thought Hamish. I really hate her.

The morning dawned sunny and crisp, sunlight sparkling on the canal below the window.

They had a silent breakfast. Hamish began to feel mutinous. He did not want to stay locked up in this hotel room.

He made for the door.

'Where are you going?' demanded Olivia sharply.

'Just downstairs to get the English papers,' said Hamish mildly.

'Don't be long.'

With a feeling of being let out of some sort of prison, Hamish went downstairs and straight out of the hotel. He was aware that the two Glaswegians, who had been sitting in the hotel lobby, had risen to follow him.

He walked slowly, looking always for a way to lose his pursuers. He went into a souvenir shop. His pursuers took up a position in a doorway across the road.

'Can I help you?'

Hamish found himself looking at a very pretty blonde. She had a mass of blonde curls, bright blue eyes and a voluptuous figure in cut-off jeans and a shirt tied at her waist.

'Just looking,' said Hamish. She smiled at him. She had dimples. Hamish stared at her.

'What is the matter?' she asked in a prettily accented voice.

'I was thinking I hadn't seen dimples in a long while,' said Hamish.

'Dimples? What is that?'

'Those indentations in your face when you smile.'

'You like?' she asked flirtatiously.

'I like.' He smiled down at her. 'Is this your shop?'

'No, I do not normally work here but I am helping out my friend, who has gone for coffee. I am a student.'

Hamish looked at her thoughtfully. 'Is there a back way out of here?'

'Yes, but why?'

'It's my wife. She's an awfy bully. I gave her the slip. I wanted to see a bit of Amsterdam but she wants to stay in the hotel room. She's got her brother following me.'

The girl laughed. 'And why should I help you?'

'Because you've got a bonny face.'

'Bonny?'

'It's Scottish for pretty.'

'Here is my friend. Greta, we're just going out the back way.'

Greta said something in Dutch and Hamish's new friend replied rapidly in the same language. Greta appeared to be lecturing the girl to be careful but she shrugged and said to Hamish in English, 'This way.'

She held up a curtain at the back of the shop. Hamish ducked his head and went through. There was a sort of back parlour-cum-kitchen and a glass door leading out into a sunny courtyard.

'We cycle,' she said.

'You're coming with me?'

'I show you some of Amsterdam, yes? I am Anna.' She held out a small hand.

'Hamish.'

'Haymeesh? What sort of name is that?'

'It's Highland, Scottish for James.'

'I love the Scots. So we go.'

They wheeled bicycles out into a narrow cobbled street which ran along by a canal. She pedalled off and Hamish, with a feeling of exhilaration, mounted and pedalled after her.

'I do not know what you are talking about,' said Greta, facing the two Glaswegians. 'My friend Anna went off with her friend.'

The one called Sammy thrust his face close to Greta's and said menacingly, 'You'd better tell us, hen.'

Greta pressed an alarm button under the counter and took a step back. 'I do not know what you are or what you want,' she said. 'Get out of here.'

The alarm button was not only connected to the local police station, but lit up a warning light outside the door of the shop, which, unknown to the two Glaswegians, was flashing like a beacon.

So that just as Sammy was about to utter further threats, suddenly there were four very large Dutch policemen in the shop

Greta spoke in rapid Dutch. The Glaswegians were handcuffed and led off. One policeman waited behind and took a statement from Greta. 'It's Anna,' said Greta ruefully. 'I don't know who the man is she went off with. He was very tall, with flaming-red hair. British.'

Water, water, everywhere, thought Hamish as Anna's delectable rump bobbed on the bicycle in front of him. They shot down cobbled streets, each one looking remarkably like the other, and then along the banks of yet another canal until Anna stopped in front of a tall building.

'I live up there,' she said. 'Coffee?'

Hamish's spurt of rebellion was beginning to fade. Olivia's cold and angry face rose in his mind's eye. But, *hey*, he was supposed to be in charge of the operation.

Olivia was pacing up and down in front of Pieter. 'What do I do now?' she asked. 'He's been gone for ages. They may have killed him.'

'I shouldn't think so,' said Pieter. 'I'll go off and check with my contacts with the police.'

Hamish was sitting by a sunny window in Anna's kitchen, sipping coffee and enjoying the *foreignness* of it all. The very coffee he was drinking tasted foreign and exotic.

'Hamish!' Anna's voice calling from another room.

He got to his feet. 'Where are you?'

'In here.'

He looked into the living room: heavy carved fruitwood furniture, canary in a cage by the window, tall dresser with thick pottery blue-and-white mugs and plates.

'Hamish!'

He pushed open a door. The bedroom. Anna lying on the bed, naked.

'Come here.' She held out her hand.

'I haff n-not the p-protection,' he said, but approached the bed all the same, gazing at the ripe young body as if hypnotized.

She turned away from him and jerked open the drawer of a bedside table. 'Help yourself.'

Hamish moved round the large double bed and looked down into the drawer. Piles of condoms.

'I d-don't think ...' he began, but she reached up and wrapped her arms around his neck.

'We have a little fun ... yes?'

How long had he been gone? wondered Olivia. He had left at nine in the morning and it was now approaching two in the afternoon. No word from Pieter. What should she do? She was feeling guilty. She knew she had treated him with unusual coldness. Soon, she would need to phone Strathbane and tell them what had happened. Then Pieter's discreet inquiries would be no good. There would need to be a full-scale police search for Hamish Macbeth.

There was a knock at the door. 'Hamish!' she cried, and ran to open it. But it was Pieter who stood there.

'Any news?'

'Yes.'

'Is he alive?'

'Very much so.'

'What happened?'

'They have video cameras at about every street corner in central Amsterdam. By running back the film of the street corners near the hotel for about the time you said Hamish disappeared, we saw him leave. He went into a souvenir shop. The woman said he had gone off with her friend Anna, who sometimes minds the shop for her. They left by the back way. The two Glaswegians came in and threatened her. She pressed the alarm bell and got them arrested. They have been told they are not welcome in Holland and sent on their way. I told the police at a high level that arresting them would complicate our business here.'

'But this Anna . . .?'

'She's a prostitute. Friend Greta tried to claim she was just a girl who likes a good time. But she's on the books. She does have a good time but she takes money for it. I wonder what excuse our friend Hamish will have when he eventually shows up.'

Hamish Macbeth awoke from a deep sleep. He felt marvellous. Then he looked at the clock. Two in the afternoon?

He hurriedly got into his clothes. He shook Anna awake. 'I've got to go.'

She smiled up at him. 'I'll have another sleep. Just leave the money on the table.'

Hamish's mouth dropped open.

'I take sterling,' she said cheerfully. 'Fifty pounds.'

Hamish fished out his wallet. Anna had closed her beautiful eyes again.

Vanity, vanity, he thought dismally. And I thought you fancied me. At least he was carrying around enough money in his role of drug baron. He peeled off the money and put it down on the table.

He made his way down the narrow dark staircase and stood outside blinking in the sunlight. He didn't know where he was. How on earth was he going to explain his absence? Perhaps he could say that he had given the Glaswegians the slip and then turned and followed *them*, to see if they contacted anyone. That would do.

He walked and walked down cobbled streets and along by canals until he saw a taxi and hailed it. 'Hilton,' he said, and lay back in the cab, thinking all the while of Olivia's angry face.

He used his own key to let himself into the hotel room.

Pieter and Olivia were sitting in armchairs. They looked up at him, waiting, waiting, and with that Highland sixth sense of his, he all at once knew that somehow *they* knew not only where he had been but what he had been doing.

'Where have you been?' asked Olivia.

Hamish pulled up another chair and sat down. Nothing but the truth would serve.

'I've been making a fool of myself.' He sighed. 'It wass like this. I felt confined in here. I've never been abroad before and I thought the only part of Amsterdam I'm going to see is this hotel room and maybe the odd restaurant or nightclub. I only meant to walk around for a bit. I went into a souvenir shop around the corner and I met this girl. I could see the Glaswegians across the road and wanted to give them the slip. She led me out the back way, lent me a bicycle and asked me to follow her and I did. We went to her flat. I didn't know she was a prostitute until she demanded payment. I paid her and came back.'

'And this is what I'm supposed to be working with,' said Olivia to Pieter. 'The village idiot abroad. I'd better phone Strathbane and abort the whole business. This man –' she jerked a contemptuous thumb at Hamish – 'is going to get us all killed.'

Pieter repressed a smile. He had expected Hamish to tell some highly embroidered lie. The fact that Hamish had told nothing but the truth amused him. Also Pieter found Olivia's dictatorial manner irritating. Men must stick together against bullying women. Poor Olivia, had she been a man, Pieter would have backed her all the way.

'I think that Strathbane would be furious with you for aborting an already expensive operation,' said Pieter smoothly, 'and as you are in charge of this case, it is you who would look bad, not Hamish here.'

Olivia felt suddenly weary. Oh, what it was to be a woman! Hamish would emerge as a bit of a lad and she would emerge as a carping bitch.

'I shall never forgive you for this,' she snapped at Hamish. 'But Pieter has a point. A lot of money has already been paid out on this. But from now on you will obey orders and do as you are told.'

'Yes, ma'am,' said Hamish meekly.

Pieter took his leave and said he would collect them later for the nightclub.

'Don't you know a prostitute when you see one?' demanded Olivia. 'What kind of copper are you?'

Hamish had suffered enough. He rose to his feet.

'If you will excuse me, ma'am, I will go to my room.'

He walked stiffly past her, his face flaming as red as his hair, and, ignoring her shout of 'It's my room, too', he went into the bedroom and shut the door behind him.

He threw himself down on the bed and stared at the ceiling. Prostitutes in Strathbane were raddled middle-aged women or pallid young girls with so many needle marks on their arms they looked like pincushions. And even that damns me as a fogey, thought Hamish. When did anyone last see a pincushion? How was he supposed to know that a fresh-looking young girl who was helping out in a souvenir shop was a prostitute? She had been warm and generous and loving. He had thought his dreams had come true. He remembered that just before he fell asleep, he had imagined her in the kitchen of the police station in Lochdubh, busy among the cooking pots, her canary singing in a cage by the window.

He felt almost tearful with shame.

Olivia was on the telephone to headquarters in Strathbane, using the mobile phone. Much as she would have liked to shop Hamish, to put in an official complaint, she was well aware that it would be the end of the operation. She would save the gem about Hamish and the prostitute for her final report. Mr Daviot listened to her report about how they had laid the ground, that they were going to a night-club tonight to set the scene. Then she said, 'We were followed by two of Jimmy White's goons but they got arrested for harassing some woman in a shop. So I do not see any reason why we should stay here any longer than tonight, running up expensive hotel bills.'

'I will rely on your judgement,' said Daviot, who had a slight crush on Olivia. 'So we can expect you back tomorrow?'

'Yes, I'll make the travel arrangements.'

She said goodbye and then collected her own and Hamish's airline tickets from her bag

171

and phoned the airline and booked them both out on an early flight in the morning. Hamish Macbeth would be easier to control on home ground.

'Good morning, sir,' said Chief Inspector Blair as he met Mr Daviot in one of the long dreary lime-green corridors of police headquarters in Strathbane.

'Ah, good morning. Mrs Daviot thanks you very much for the flowers. Fancy you remembering her birthday.'

'Just a little something. Everything going well over there?'

'Things seem to be running smoothly so far. I hope Macbeth realizes at last that he has potential. He's too bright to be locked away in a Highland village.'

Blair nodded and walked on. He had a pounding headache, having drunk too much the night before. He seethed at the idea of Hamish Macbeth getting any glory at all. Would it be so terrible to drop a word in the wrong quarters? They wouldn't kill Hamish, just probably disappear back to Glasgow. It would not be as if he, Blair, would be thwarting the police and Customs and Excise from seizing a valuable cargo. The cargo was a scam.

He would never be found out. All it would take was one little whisper.

* * *

Hamish received the news of their impending departure calmly. He had lost all his resentment to Olivia. He was so ashamed of himself that he actually now welcomed her cold, brisk efficiency.

Olivia had put on less make-up that evening. She was wearing a brief black evening dress with gold jewellery. Her hair was down on her shoulders, smooth and shining.

'You look very well,' said Hamish awkwardly as he helped her into her coat.

She threw him a brief smile. 'I thought I was beginning to look a bit too vulgar.'

Pieter called to collect them and they all set off for the nightclub.

The nightclub was dark, with candles on the tables. 'I don't know how anyone's even going to see us here,' he murmured to Pieter.

'The cabaret's about to begin,' said Pieter. 'We're near the front and the lights from the stage will show us clearly. We'll just need to hope your Glaswegians have been replaced.'

'There was that chap with them, the one I saw in Lachie's office, the one I call the Undertaker,' said Hamish. 'He'll still be around. If he's not here himself, he'll send someone else.'

Suddenly the stage was lit up and the compère dashed on. He spoke in rapid Dutch and then German and English. Lola was to be the first turn, a lady of renowned international beauty. The audience laughed and Hamish wondered what was so funny about that.

Then Lola came on, a statuesque blonde with enormous breasts and high cheekbones. In a Marlene Dietrich voice, she started to sing 'Falling in Love Again'. Hamish realized with a little shock that Lola was a man. The wrists and ankles were always a giveaway.

'That's a man,' whispered Olivia to Hamish.

'I know,' he said crossly, thinking she really must consider him some sort of dumb hayseed, and then he remembered she had every reason to consider him an innocent abroad.

After Lola had finished, the lights blazed out from the stage as she began to sing 'I Will Survive'.

Hamish glanced covertly around. Just sitting down, a few tables behind him, was Anna, accompanied by a heavy-set businessman.

Pieter followed his gaze. 'That's your lady of today,' he said.

'How do you know?' asked Hamish, raising his voice to be heard above Lola's singing.

Pieter leaned forward and told him about the street videos.

'I feel a right fool,' said Hamish. 'Does she have a pimp?'

'No, she's a bit of an enthusiastic amateur. But any day now, someone's going to take her over. She's only been busted once. She tried to pick up a businessman in a hotel and his wife phoned the police. That's the only reason she came to their notice. Cheer up, Hamish. It was an easy mistake to make.'

174

Olivia, who had overheard the conversation, studied Anna. Anna looked as fresh and wholesome as newly baked bread. She could easily have passed for her escort's daughter. She could all at once understand why Hamish had made such a mistake.

Lola departed the stage in a flurry of ostrich feathers and sequins. She was replaced by a conjuror. The audience promptly ignored what was happening on the stage and the babble of voices rose.

'Our American friends have just come in.' Pieter waved. 'And there's a thin man in a black suit leaning against a pillar at the back. Take a look, Hamish, and see if you recognize him.'

'Which pillar? Where?'

'At the back, to the left of the exit.'

Hamish looked and then looked quickly away. 'It's the Undertaker, Lachie's man. I wonder why he's so obvious. He must know I would recognize him.'

'They probably want you to know you're being checked up on. Good. Then on the way out, we'll stop at various tables.'

'Surely these drug people will be mighty suspicious of anyone muscling in on their territory.'

'Amsterdam is not their home ground, not the ones you'll meet. They're here to see to shipments.'

The conjuror finished his act to a spattering of applause.

'How long do we sit here for?' asked Olivia, ignoring the compère's patter. 'I'm getting bored.'

'Just a little longer,' said Pieter.

'I'm hungry,' complained Olivia. 'I haven't had any dinner.'

'And I didn't have any lunch either,' said Hamish.

'No, you were eating the fair Anna,' said Pieter, and laughed.

'Cut that out, now,' snapped Olivia. 'Remember Hamish is supposed to be my husband. I don't like coarseness.'

'Then don't look at the stage,' said Hamish.

But Olivia looked. Two men and a woman were engaged in complicated sexual acts.

'Aren't you enjoying it?' she asked Hamish.

'I'm not a voyeur,' said Hamish, averting his eyes from the stage. Pieter ordered more drinks after the cavorting threesome had been replaced by semi-naked showgirls. Hamish sipped his drink cautiously. He was beginning to feel the effects of champagne on an empty stomach.

'I think we should leave now,' said Olivia, much to Hamish's relief.

They all rose. As Hamish passed Anna's table, she looked up at him and gave him a glad smile.

Hamish cut her dead. He was supposed to be with his wife. Also she had left him with a bill for fifty pounds, which he would somehow have to explain away on his expenses. Anna's face fell. Hamish felt like a heel. But didn't the silly girl know what an awful sort of existence she was on the threshold of?

Pieter stopped by the Americans' table. Then he introduced them to a party of Turks and then some Spaniards before leading them towards the exit. There was no sign of the Undertaker.

'Do you know,' said Pieter outside, 'how the Spaniards are shipping cannabis into Britain?'

'No,' said Olivia.

'They put the cannabis resin into onions. So when Customs and Excise see a truckload of onions, they simply look for the man with the dart.'

'The dart?' asked Hamish, his eyes roaming up and down the cobbled street.

'A man carrying an ordinary dart, you know, darts? Like in English pubs? Well, he simply stabs this dart into the sacks of onions until he finds the hard onions and he knows he's got the right sack.'

Olivia shivered. 'Let's eat.'

'I'll take you back to your hotel. Probably safer for you to eat in your room. I have business.'

He flagged down a cab and gave the driver instructions. Hamish looked wistfully out at

177

the night lights of Amsterdam. 'I wish we didn't have to eat in the hotel.'

'We'd best do as we're told,' said Olivia. 'What a cold night it's turned out to be.'

Hamish noticed that her attitude towards him had thawed.

Once in the room, they ordered steaks to be sent up. Olivia switched on the television set and they ate and watched the news. Then they watched an American sitcom and drank coffee and there was a friendly atmosphere between them when they both went to bed. Hamish smiled in the darkness. Soon it would all be over. Soon he would be back at his police station.

Rain was drumming down on the car park at Inverness Airport when they arrived. They got into the Mercedes and Hamish set off on the drive back to Strathbane. 'So do we just wait out the rest of the week?' he asked.

'I think we should try to speed things up,' said Olivia. 'We'll go and see Lachie tomorrow and tell him to tell Jimmy that the consignment is on its way.'

For some reason, Hamish suddenly found his thoughts turning in the direction of Chief Inspector Blair. He wondered if Blair had got wind of what he was up to. He knew Blair hated him.

'I'll be glad when this is over,' said Olivia suddenly.

'Why?'

'I don't know. I've got a bad feeling about it. Things have been running a bit too easily, apart from your gaffe in Amsterdam.'

'I'm sorry about that,' said Hamish ruefully. 'I thought I had landed lucky at last. I could even see us married. I would never have believed I could be so naive. If you see any of the prostitutes in Strathbane, well, they've practically got labels round their necks screaming prostitute. I meet the girl of my dreams and then she says, "Leave the money on the table as you go out."'

'Pieter did say she was a happy amateur, but she won't be happy for long.'

'She told me she was a student.'

'Student of what?' commented Olivia dryly. 'A lot of these silly girls just drift into it. It can start with a simple date with an older man. He gets the wrong end of the stick and pays up. Girl is mortified, then she giggles about it a bit with her friends, and the money comes in handy. Who knows? Maybe Anna was a student, and recently, too. It seems a harmless way of making a bit of money on the side. Some pimp starts to sit up and take notice. He acts as the john, introduces her to dope, gets her hooked and then puts her on the street.'

'Perhaps she'll just stop.'

'I doubt it. Are you so lonely, Hamish, that you should want to marry some girl you had just met?'

'I suppose I'm a romantic.'

'You're in the wrong job. A lot of the men down in Glasgow consider me cold and harsh, but I have found that any sign of softness is taken as a come-on.'

'I'm glad I'm not a woman,' said Hamish, negotiating a hairpin bend.

There was a companionable silence and then he said, 'I wasn't making a pass at you in the bed at the Grand. I really wasn't.'

'I believe you, but I'll get us a room with twin beds this time so there will be no ... awkwardness.'

'You were saying you had a bad feeling about this job,' said Hamish. 'You know something? I cannae help worrying that too many people at headquarters know about it.'

'Only the top brass, surely.'

It's the top brass I'm worried about, thought Hamish.

Chapter Seven

Our fears do make us traitors.
– William Shakespeare

The following day, Hamish and Olivia held a secret meeting with Chief Superintendent Daviot and Kevin and Barry on the moors high above Strathbane.

'We have decided on a further cunning plan,' began Daviot. Hamish suppressed a groan. 'We have a yacht registered to you, Hamish, the *Marie-Claire*, a ketch. She will only be carrying one kilo of heroin. This, you will say, is to prove the quality of the stuff and to make sure the landing place is safe. We will let that deal go through. Then you will promise the rest of the shipment. They will be lulled into a false sense of security. On the second delivery, that is when we will pounce.'

'I don't like the delay,' said Hamish. 'I'm always frightened that the longer we wait, the more chance there is of word leaking out that the whole thing is a scam.'

'Chief Inspector Chater?' asked Daviot.

'It sounds all right to me,' said Olivia. 'With so few people knowing about it, I can't see anything going wrong. We're going to Lachie's tonight. When will we say the first shipment is due to arrive?'

'Say two days' time. That should speed things up enough for you, Macbeth.' Not 'Hamish' this time. The super was obviously disappointed in what he saw as Hamish's sad lack of enthusiasm.

'Very well, sir,' said Olivia. 'We will do what we can.'

'Let's hope the weather's all right,' said Hamish. 'Who will be skippering the ketch?'

'A police officer from Inverness. And the crew are policemen as well.'

'Will they be armed?' asked Hamish.

Daviot looked at him impatiently. 'There will be no need for that. Jimmy White will not be expecting them to be around.'

'On the contrary, sir. I would think that any drug baron would expect a crew bringing in heroin to be armed.'

'I don't believe in guns,' said Daviot severely. 'Guile is the answer. Just do your part, Macbeth, and leave the rest to Chief Inspector Chater.'

'Won't it look odd my wife going along as well?' asked Hamish.

'You'll think of something,' said Daviot crossly. Why couldn't Macbeth show some *enthusiasm*? 'You can hardly leave the senior officer on the case behind.'

What was that American phrase? thought Hamish. Amateur night in Dixie, this was it.

'And what do we do when we know the landing place?' asked Hamish.

'Olivia will contact us. The first shipment, we will have men observing. The second shipment we'll seize them.'

'Very good, sir,' said Hamish in a hollow voice.

'Well, I'll be on my way.' Daviot cast a stagy look around the moors. 'Coast's clear.'

Hamish watched his retreating figure. 'Now I know why so many top policemen are Freemasons,' he said 'They like playing games.'

'Show respect,' snapped Olivia.

'I don't like it at all,' said Hamish wearily.

Olivia suppressed a qualm of unease. She had, she remembered, considered the whole business at the beginning quite mad. 'We've got our orders,' she said briskly. 'We'll go to Lachie's tonight.'

They entered Lachie's that evening, flanked by Kevin and Barry. 'I see Bob over there,' said Hamish. 'I wonder why he didn't demand payment for the introduction.'

'He did,' said Olivia. 'Kevin paid him out of the kitty when you were in with Jimmy White.'

They asked at the bar for Lachie, and after a short wait, the Undertaker appeared.

'Enjoy your stay in Amsterdam?' asked Hamish.

The Undertaker gave a thin smile. 'We always check up. Lachie's waiting.'

Lachie rose to meet them when they walked into the office.

'Great to see you, Hamish, my man. I think we should have a wee talk in private. Your lady and friends can wait at the bar.'

'My wife is my business partner,' said Hamish. 'She stays.'

Hamish slung his coat from his shoulders and sat down after pulling out a chair for Olivia. 'I think the time has come when we prove our good faith to each other. My boat will land a kilo of heroin. You name the place, you check the quality. If all goes well, we'll land the rest of the stuff at a second meet.'

'Right you are,' said Lachie. 'Jimmy'll be up from Glasgow tomorrow. Meet him here about the same time. Let's have a drink. On the house.'

'Verra kind,' said Hamish, his accent becoming more Highland with nerves. 'But we haff urgent business to attend to.'

He stood up and slung his coat over his shoulders.

'Aye, see you,' said Lachie, although his eyes slid curiously to Olivia.

* * *

Back in the hotel room, Hamish said, 'You should have kept your tarty image, Olivia. Lachie found it odd that you should be my business partner.'

Olivia was wearing a tailored suit and subdued make-up. 'Also,' Hamish went on, 'you've got to act the part from the inside out. You were emanating an atmosphere of senior police officer, Olivia. It's a wonder he didn't look down to see if you had big boots on.'

'You're the one who has to act the part,' said Olivia.

'He's right,' said Kevin. 'I thought myself you were looking a bit severe.'

Olivia capitulated. 'Oh, well, I'll do better tomorrow night.'

'Fancy a drink in the bar downstairs, Hamish?' said Barry.

'Aye, that would be grand.'

'I have some phone calls to make,' said Olivia. 'You go ahead.'

'It's the first time I've seen plastic tartan,' said Hamish, sitting down on a tartan banquette. 'Isn't this hotel awful?'

'The whole of Strathbane is awful,' said Kevin. 'All that lovely highland countryside all about and this town sitting in the middle of it like some great excrescence.'

They ordered whiskies. 'The thing that's bothering me,' said Barry, leaning forward, 'is that Superintendent Daviot. He's like a wee boy playing at cops and robbers. And the men on the boat ought to be armed.'

'Aye,' said Hamish. 'I don't like this idea of two shipments. One would have nailed them, quicker and safer. Olivia's not stupid. Why didn't she object?'

'Because she got where she is today,' said Kevin, 'by agreeing with everything the higher ranks said or told her to do. And it's landed her in some hairy situations before. She knows if she starts sticking pins in Daviot's plans, then he'll report her as an officer who is awkward to work with.'

Hamish looked around the bar. He was wearing his dark glasses just in case he saw a familiar face, but there were few people in that night.

He stayed talking to Kevin and Barry for about an hour and then they all went upstairs to their respective rooms.

'You took your time,' said Olivia when he walked in. 'And you smell of whisky. I hope you're not turning out to be a drunk.'

'I only had a couple,' protested Hamish. 'I can nurse a drink for a pretty long time.'

'Why is it always just a couple? That's the sign of a drunk, Hamish.'

Hamish repressed a sigh. Frosty Olivia was back again.

The fact was that Olivia was as nervous as Hamish over the forthcoming operation, but could not confide in him. She had got this far in police ranks by never criticizing a superior officer to anyone.

'Chust a suggestion,' said Hamish tentatively.

'That being?'

'I didn't like the look in Lachie's eyes when I said you were my business partner. We're going to have to look as if we're in love.'

'Why?'

'Well, it figures that a man who was besotted with his wife would take her everywhere.'

She sat frowning for a moment and then said, 'All right. We'll try that.'

'Do you know what it's like to be in love, Olivia?'

To his surprise, her face flamed scarlet and she said, 'Mind your own business.'

'Sorry. Look, are we going to have to stay cooped up in here tomorrow? Or can we go somewhere?'

'Where?'

'Anywhere. We could take a picnic. The weather forecast says it's going to be fine and there won't be many more fine days. Winter sets in early up here.'

'I'll check with Daviot tomorrow. I don't see any reason why we can't go out.'

Hamish brightened. 'I'll buy some stuff for a picnic tomorrow morning.'

'No, you won't,' said Olivia sharply. 'Drug barons don't go out shopping for picnics. We'll send Kevin and Barry. I don't think we need to take them with us, though. We're not in any danger.'

'Yet,' said Hamish, but she had reached over and switched on the television set and did not hear.

The following day they set off with a generous hamper of goodies in the back seat, Kevin having done the shopping at Strathbane's one posh delicatessen.

'Where are we going?' asked Olivia as the sun sparkled on the broken glass in front of one of Strathbane's many dismal high-rises.

'The Falls of Braggie. It's a beauty spot.'

'Won't it be full of tourists?'

'Too late in the year.'

The Falls of Braggie, a tremendous waterfall of gold peaty water, crashed down from a great height. Rainbows danced in the spray. Ferns already turning golden lined the steep banks of the River Braggie. Rowan trees heavy with dark red berries stood gracefully on the banks.

'Is there any sort of flat place round here?' asked Olivia.

'There,' said Hamish, pointing to a flat rock in the middle of the river below the falls.

'And how do we get across?'

'There's some rocks that act as stepping-stones. I'll leave the car here and then we'll carry the hamper down to the river.'

'What on earth has Kevin bought?' groaned Olivia as they edged their way down, carrying the heavy hamper between them. 'Half the shop?'

When they got to the edge of the river, she noticed there was a little causeway of rocks leading out to the flat stone. They gingerly made their way across and sat down with the hamper between them, the sun hot on their heads.

Olivia lifted the lid. 'Now, let's see what we have here. Good God, what a waste of police money!'

There was cold grouse, pâté, rolls and butter, salad, various cheeses, chocolate cake and among various other goodies a bottle of vintage champagne.

'I think Kevin was just trying to keep up our rich image,' said Hamish. 'Let me see. Did he put in glasses to drink out of? No, he didn't, silly man. We'll need to drink out of the bottle.'

'Not you. You're driving.'

'I'll have a mouthful. Oh, look, here's a flask of coffee and paper cups. We can use the cups.'

'This is incredibly beautiful,' said Olivia, looking around her. 'I'm beginning to understand why you love it up here so much.'

'He's remembered plates and knives and forks,' said Hamish, rummaging in the bottom of the hamper. 'Do you want me to serve?'

'No, I'll do it. I'm not completely de-feminized.'

Olivia was wearing trousers, and a sky-blue lambswool sweater over a blue silk blouse. Hamish was wearing an expensive sports shirt and designer jeans. 'I wonder what happens to all these clothes when I hand them back,' he said, watching Olivia as she arranged squares of pâté, Melba toast and pats of butter on two plates.

'They probably go back into some sort of police wardrobe. Oh, open the champagne. We may as well have a glass, or rather a paper cup, of the stuff.'

Hamish filled two cups and then placed the bottle carefully in the shallow water which ran round the rock to keep cool.

'I can't believe it's so warm,' said Olivia.

'It's the lack of pollution up here,' replied Hamish. 'The sun has nothing to block the rays. It'll be cold tonight, mind, with a sharp frost.'

'There speaks the true countryman. What's the matter?'

There was a sudden wariness and stillness about Hamish.

'I don't think we're alone. Don't look round!'

'How do you know?'

'Chust a feeling.'

'Probably tourists,' said Olivia impatiently.

'Now we start to flirt,' said Hamish. 'Voices carry.'

He raised his voice. 'More champagne, darling?' He lowered his voice. 'And take that suspicious look off your face. I am not using this as an excuse to make a pass at you.'

'That would be lovely,' said Olivia loudly. 'If you've finished your pâté, we'll start on this grouse.'

Hamish smiled at her lazily and glanced idly around. His sharp eyes caught a flash of light up on the left bank. 'We're being watched through binoculars. I'm going to kiss you.'

'Is that necessary? Married men don't go around kissing their wives in public.'

'Besotted ones do. Lean forward and pucker up.'

Olivia leaned forward. His kiss was warm and gentle and strangely comforting. He shifted around the rock and gathered her in his arms. 'Don't go too far,' she whispered.

'I won't.' He kissed her again. She relaxed against him. She began to return his kisses, feeling warm and languid in the sun, both of them forgetting the watcher, both of them locked in a little world far from drugs and danger.

Hamish stole a quick look up the hill. No flash from binoculars, but then through a screen of rowan trees, he saw a black car moving off. He wanted to go on kissing her but he knew his sensual pleasure in the feel of her lips and the feel of her body against his was slowly turning to passion.

'Our watcher has gone, Olivia,' he said. 'We can carry on eating.'

She moved away from him and bent her head over the hamper. Her cheeks were flushed and her bosom rose and fell.

'I hope you realize that was all in the line of duty, Hamish.'

'It was a pleasant duty, ma'am. Do you like grouse? I'll tell you about a famous grouse race where two men competed to see who could get the first brace of grouse of the season to London first and how it led to murder.'

Olivia listened, grateful to Hamish for having easily got over what might have been an awkwardness.

When he had finished his story, she handed him a plate of grouse and said, 'Who do you think was watching us?'

'Probably the Undertaker or one of Jimmy White's henchmen.'

'I don't like it. They should not be so suspicious of us now.'

'We're still an unknown quantity,' said Hamish. 'Let's talk about something else.'

'Like what?'

'When I asked you if you'd ever been in love, you fair bit my head off. Why was that?'

'I'll tell you. If only to make sure you don't talk to the lads about snogging with a chief inspector.'

She ate a mouthful of grouse. Then she said, 'I was a detective constable, young, ambitious.

He was a chief inspector called Fergus Shane. He was handsome and clever. At first I had a crush on him, that was all, you know, like a schoolgirl crush. Then one evening I had been working late on a case and I had just filed my report when he came in. He asked me if I had eaten and when I said I hadn't had the time, he took me out for dinner. Over the first dinner, he told me he was married. That cooled me down. After that, a few weeks passed and again I was working late and again he asked me out for dinner. He said his wife was away visiting her sister in Elgin. It seemed like just a friendly invitation.'

The sun went behind a cloud and there was a sudden chill in the air. She shivered and hugged her knees. 'He told me he was getting a divorce. There were no children and nothing to tie him down. And then he said he had fallen in love with me, and I believed him. By the end of that dinner, I was head over heels in love. We began an affair in secret. He said it had to be secret until the divorce came through.

'And then I came back to the station late one night. I had been out on a case which had fallen through. I wasn't expected back at all, but I thought I may as well get my report out of the way. I saw the light shining through the frosted glass of his door and my heart lifted. Then I heard the sound of masculine laughter. I hesitated outside the door, wondering who was with him and whether to go in, when I heard a man say, "So what's our Olivia like in bed, Fergus?"

'And then the voice of my beloved came loud and clear, "Hot stuff. Bit naive. Screams a lot. *Fergus, oh, Fergus*, that sort of thing."'

She fell silent, staring at the rushing river.

'So what did you do?' asked Hamish.

'I went to my flat. I wanted to die of shame. But I wanted revenge. I could not report him, of course, I couldn't. If I told his wife, then I would lose my job. All the men would be on his side. Then I thought that if he had done it to me, he would do it to someone else. First I dropped him. I told him I was seeing someone else. I had a nasty time after that, all the rotten cases, but I waited and watched. The chief superintendent's old bat of a secretary retired and he got a new one, very pretty girl in a hard sort of bitchy way. I saw Fergus beginning to sniff round her. I watched and waited. I began to follow them. I got a camera. I took pictures of them in restaurants and then I followed them when they went to Rothesay for the day and got some tremendous snaps of them kissing on the beach.

'I sent the photographs to his wife and another set to the chief superintendent.'

'What happened to him?'

'Nothing would have happened on the job front, I suppose, except that the secretary told the super that Fergus had not told her he was married and had promised to marry her. He had even given her a ring. Then the wife arrived, screaming blue murder. He was demoted and transferred to a small local police station. He left the police force and is now, I believe, chief security officer at a big chemical works. I'm not proud of what I did. I haven't been with a man since.'

'It's a wonder you didn't leave the force yourself,' said Hamish.

'I threw myself into my work. I got the reputation of being a hard woman. God, I don't know why I told you all this.'

'Have some champagne. I havenae been lucky in love either.'

Feeling that one confidence deserved another, Hamish refilled her cup, and told her about his aborted love affair with Priscilla Halburton-Smythe. 'In fact, I never have much luck with women,' he said ruefully. 'Anna in Amsterdam was a typical mess-up. It's getting cold. I think we should go.'

Kevin whispered to Barry as they walked into Lachie's that night, 'Something's going on between that pair.' He jerked a thumb at Olivia and Hamish.

'Oh, that. Hamish told me that they're pretending to be mad about each other,' muttered Barry, 'so that Jimmy won't think it odd her going along on the drop.'

'Good act if you ask me,' said Kevin, shouldering his way ahead.

Once more into Lachie's office. 'Well, Hamish,' cried Jimmy White. 'I gather you've got an idea we should check a wee bit o' the load.'

'Aye, that way you can see the stuff is good and I can be sure you're not about to double-cross me,' sneered Hamish, his arm around Olivia's shoulders.

'Oh, come on, man, all friends here.'

'If that's the case, you can tell that lang dreep o' a man over there,' Hamish said, pointing to the Undertaker, 'to stop following me around.'

'It's no' my man. That's Lachie. Suspicious o' his ain mither. Right, to business.'

One of Jimmy's men spread out an ordnance survey map. 'We would like you to land the stuff here in two days' time. Can you manage that?'

Hamish looked at the map. Of all the damn places, he thought. Loch Drim!

'Why there?'

'One of our spies said it was a grand place to land. We havenae used it before. Your men bring the stuff ashore to this point.' He stabbed down on the rocky promontory opposite the cave where Jock had hidden his monster.

'But to get there you'll have to go through the village of Drim,' said Hamish, 'and believe me, the locals will know you're there.'

'No, they won't. You'll be coming in my boat and we'll go in from the sea as well.'

'In that case, why not go out to my boat and pick the stuff up at sea?' demanded Hamish.

'Could be caught by the Customs and Excise that way. My boat will drop us there one hour before the meet. I assume your lads have the stuff well hidden. If the Customs come cruising around, they won't bother much with one boat, but two together would excite their suspicions.'

I hope Jock's given up playing with his monster, thought Hamish.

'Well, Hamish?' demanded Jimmy. 'Can you get the stuff there in two days' time? That'll be Monday morning at two a.m.'

Hamish thought quickly. He was sure that for this operation the ketch would have a high-powered engine.

'It's a deal,' he said, holding out his hand.

Jimmy shook it, and then, holding on to Hamish's hand, looked at the calluses on it which Hamish had got from working round the croft.

'Done time?' he asked.

'South America,' said Hamish, pulling his hand away. 'Bribed my way out.'

'Okay, let's have a drink,' said Jimmy.

Fortunately for Hamish, Jimmy liked to brag rather than listen. He told of drug deals and contacts. Hamish felt himself go almost weak with relief. Jimmy trusted them.

But he only breathed easily when they got out of there and back to the hotel.

'Can we start writing down what he said?' Kevin looked anxious. 'All those names, all those drug contacts.'

Olivia laughed and unbuttoned her blouse. Underneath, she was wearing a brief lacy bra and in her cleavage was tucked a little black tape recorder. 'Got every word,' she said.

'Very good, ma'am,' said Hamish curtly as Kevin and Barry goggled. 'I think you can cover yourself up now.'

Olivia turned a faint shade of pink as she quickly buttoned up her blouse. 'I'm going to try this out and phone Daviot,' she said.

She went off into the bedroom. 'Anything going on between you two?' asked Kevin. On the other side of the bedroom door, Olivia pressed her ear to the panel.

'Don't be silly,' she heard Hamish say clearly. 'She's a good officer and I've forgotten she's a woman.'

'With boobs like that!' exclaimed Kevin.

'You chust forget she's a woman as well,' snapped Hamish.

Olivia moved away, grateful to Hamish for keeping quiet about their afternoon on the rock. She phoned Daviot.

Hamish lay awake a long time that night, not because Olivia was lying in the bed beside his, but because he was now worried about Jock Kennedy and his monster. But Jock would know that one more sighting of his rubber beastie would bring Hamish down on his head. So much to worry about, thought Hamish. Jimmy had said he would pick them up at their hotel on Sunday evening. Nothing he could do until then but wait and worry.

Hamish and Olivia mostly kept to their hotel room. Kevin had bought them a Scrabble board and they played games and watched television and read. It seemed a long time until Sunday night but suddenly it was upon them and there was one of Jimmy's henchmen to drive them down to a high-powered boat in the oily, polluted harbour of Strathbane where even the seagulls looked dirty.

They joined Jimmy in the cabin, all sitting around the table, but not saying much. One of the crew landed them on the point at the head of Loch Drim. 'Now we wait,' said Hamish. He looked across the darkness towards the cave but there was no sound and no sign of life.

The night was frosty and calm. He had never known an hour pass so slowly. Then at last they heard the faint sound of an outboard engine.

'That should be it,' he said with an air of

relaxed ease which belied the rapid beating of his heart.

The sound of the engine approached and then cut off. There was silence apart from the lapping of the waves and then the sound of oars in rowlocks. Hamish took out a torch and gave a brief flash. There was an answering flash and then in the starlight they could see faintly a dinghy rowed by two men, pulling towards the point.

Hamish strolled forward to meet it. 'Any trouble?' he asked.

'No trouble, sir.' Hamish cursed inwardly. That 'no trouble, sir' had been a damn sight too polite and official. He took hold of the oil-skin packet the man was holding up as he stood in the rocky boat.

'Get off fast,' he ordered. 'I don't want you hanging around.'

'Yes, sir.' Damn, it's a wonder he didn't salute, thought Hamish furiously.

He turned to Jimmy. 'There's the first instalment.'

'Bring the torch here,' Jimmy ordered one of his men. He took a wicked knife out of his pocket and cut open the package and looked down at the cellophane bags.

'Aye, that'll do, Hamish. Now we wait a bit until my man comes back.'

'So if you're satisfied,' said Hamish, 'we can let you have the rest of the stuff in, say, another two days.'

200

'Aye, we'd best make it here. Say Wednesday morning. I'll pick you up same as this evening.'

'You know what I'd almost forgotten about,' said Hamish when he and Olivia were back in their hotel room. 'The person whose death started all this. Tommy Jarret. I've no doubt his parents have been trying to get hold of me. They must have thought I'd forgotten about the whole thing.'

'When we catch them, we'll sweat it out of Lachie.'

'I think such as Lachie won't talk.'

'Anyway, let's get this over with. If you like, I'll get us some time off and we can see if we can find out anything further about the boy's death. I'm going to bed. It's been a long night.'

Hamish waited until she had finished using the bathroom and then went in and ran himself a hot bath. He put on his silk pyjamas – courtesy of the police force – and went into the bedroom.

He felt his way in the darkness to his bed. He should be tired, he thought, but he was plagued by a strung-up, restless feeling mixed with an uneasy feeling of apprehension.

'Hamish.' Olivia's voice was soft in the darkness.

'Yes?'

'I can't sleep. I'm worried.'

'Me, too.'

'Hamish?'

'Yes.'

'If you come over here, we could worry together.'

'Yes, ma'am,' said Hamish Macbeth. It was the first time he had obeyed a senior officer's orders with any enthusiasm.

It was a pity that Superintendent Daviot could not tell the difference between duty and grovelling. He rated Blair highly because Blair always praised him. The temptation to boast about the latest success of the operation was too much. He sent for Blair.

'We're doing just fine,' said Daviot, rubbing his hands. 'Just fine.'

'So what's the latest, sir?'

Daviot told him about the success of the first drug delivery. 'So all we have to do is hope the second meet goes as well and then we'll have them. And Detective Chief Inspector Chater has done splendidly. When they went to Lachie's and Jimmy White was bragging about his contacts, she taped every word. We could do with someone bright like that here. We haven't got a single woman detective and it's bad for our image.'

'I think the success of the whole thing is due to your meticulous planning, sir,' said Blair.

'Well, I must say I've had a hand in it. But

give credit where it's due, I think we owe a lot to Hamish Macbeth. He's been rotting up in that village of his for too long. Drink?'

'That would be very nice, sir. Just a splash of whisky.'

Blair's mind raced. This was awful. Hamish Macbeth transferred to Strathbane was bad enough, but to have a woman of the same rank was worse. Women should stay at home and in the kitchen where they belonged.

'So you were saying,' said Blair, taking the glass of whisky handed to him, 'that the final operation is at two o'clock on Wednesday morning at the head of Loch Drim?'

'That's it and then we start a massive round-up of all the other villains. Thanks to Chater, we've got all the names.'

Blair went back to his desk afterwards and brooded over the problem. He then took out his book of informants, or snouts as they were called, and ran his finger down the list. He picked up the phone. 'Callum,' he whispered. 'Blair here. Meet me down at the Fisherman's Bar at the docks. Can you be there in an hour? There's big money in this for ye.'

He listened to the reply and then said, 'I'll see you there. Don't let me down.'

The Fisherman's Bar dated from the days when there were fishermen and the harbour at

Strathbane had been crammed with trawlers. But overfishing and European Union quotas had crippled the fishing industry and the harbour lay deserted apart from a few rusting hulks of boats. The Fisherman's Bar consisted of little more than one small smelly room. Nicotine from millions of cigarettes had stained the once-white walls yellow. There was an ancient jukebox in the corner, still containing a stack of sixties records. No one could quite remember the last time it had worked. A television set over the bar was relaying the latest horse racing from Ayr and Cheltenham. No one ever came to the bar for any good purpose. It was a haunt of small-time villains. Callum, the snout, was one of those dwarf-sized men who still inhabit inner cities. His sparse hair was combed carefully over his bald spot. He had a deeply wrinkled face, no teeth, not even false ones, to lend shape to his sour and wrinkled mouth. He wore glasses and chain-smoked.

His information was usually as small-time as the villains who used the bar – petty theft, people who grew and sold cannabis, the odd ram raid, burglary and some warehouse break-ins. He passed these tidbits on to Blair, who would pay him the occasional tenner for the information.

Blair came in and sat down at the battered table in the corner which Callum had chosen. 'I'm surprised you chose this place,' said Callum.

'Nobody knows me down here,' said Blair.

'Aye but you stink of copper,' said Callum, watching a couple of men swallow their drinks quickly and make for the door.

'Okay, we'll take a walk.' Callum looked disappointed. He craved a drink but had not ordered anything, expecting Blair to pay for one.

Both men walked out. The day was cold and clear. Mournful seagulls swooped overhead. Plastic cups, condoms, burger wrappers and other detritus bobbed on the filthy water.

'So what brings you?' asked Callum.

'This is big money,' said Blair.

'How big?'

'Very big. I'm giving you information to sell.'

Chapter Eight

O Death, where is thy sting-a-ling-a-ling,
O Grave, thy victoree?
The bells of Hell go ting-a-ling-a-ling
For you but not for me.
                                    – British army song

Callum's heart beat hard as he went into the noise of Lachie's disco that night. How much should he ask for such information? A thousand?

He went up to the bar. The bartender eyed him with disfavour. 'What d'ye want, old man?'

'Not so much o' the old man, laddie,' said Callum. 'I'm here to see Lachie.'

'Oh, aye? And what's your business?'

'I've got information for him.'

'Awa' wi' ye. He's busy.'

'Okay, tell him I'll see him in prison.' Callum had shouted the last words to be heard above the disco beat.

'Wait here,' said the bartender.

Callum turned round and watched the gyrating couples. How could folks get enjoyment out of dancing like that? The stabbing strobes hurt his eyes and the music hurt his ears. No damn tune, either.

The bartender came back. 'Come with me.'

He led Callum through to Lachie's office.

Lachie was alone. Callum threw a longing glance at the bar in the corner.

Lachie was sitting behind his desk. He did not ask Callum to sit down.

'So what's this information?' he asked.

'I'm not saying anything until I see Jimmy White and get paid for it.'

Lachie leaned forward. 'I don't know anything about anyone called Jimmy White. Get out o' here.'

'He's caught in the middle o' a police scam,' said Callum sulkily.

Lachie looked at him long and hard, and then he smiled. 'Have a seat. What's your name?'

'Callum.'

'Callum what?'

'Just Callum.'

'Drink?'

'Aye, a whisky would be fine.'

Lachie picked up the phone and, turning away from Callum, whispered into it. After he had replaced the receiver, he went to the bar and poured a generous glass of whisky for Callum.

'Cheers!' said Callum.

Lachie nodded. Then he said, 'How much are you asking for this information?'

'A thousand pounds,' said Callum.

'Well, we'll see.' The door opened and the Undertaker came in. 'On his way,' he said briefly. He sat down on a chair against the wall. He took out a nasty-looking knife and began to clean his nails.

'I thought they only did that on the fillums,' said Callum nervously. Both men said nothing, just looked steadily and unnervingly at Callum.

'It's been fine weather,' said Callum.

Nothing. They just continued to stare at him. Callum could feel sweat breaking out on his forehead. He began to curse Blair in his mind. He was beginning to feel all this was too deep and dangerous for a small-time villain like himself.

The door opened and Jimmy White came in. Callum immediately knew this must be Jimmy White from the expensive clothes and the two brutal-looking henchmen who came in behind him.

Jimmy White drew up a chair next to Callum and said, 'Speak.'

'It's important information,' said Callum. 'I want a thousand pounds for it.'

'You'll get it. Now, speak.'

'I'd like to see the money first,' said Callum, frightened but determined.

'You have the word of Jimmy White. Isn't that good enough for you?'

Callum caved in. Now all he wanted was to get out of this dreadful place. The office was soundproofed but the disco beat filtered through like the beating of his heart.

'It's like this,' he said. 'You're dealing with a man who says he's Hamish George and his wife.'

'So?'

'He's Hamish Macbeth, a copper from Lochdubh, and his so-called wife is a detective chief inspector from Glasgow. The heroin you're getting is from that haul the police grabbed in Glasgow. At the next drop, all the police will be waiting for you.'

'Who told you this?'

'I got it from top level in the police but I cannae be revealing my source. Now, what about that money?'

Jimmy White turned to one of his henchmen. He made a twisting motion with his hands. 'Pay him.'

Callum relaxed and picked up his whisky. One of the henchmen stepped forward and deftly slipped a wire around Callum's scrawny neck and pulled tight. The rest watched with interest as Callum writhed and fought and then was still. His lifeless body slumped to the floor.

'Dump that in the harbour,' said Jimmy.

'You'd best clear off,' said Lachie.

'Not before I take out Hamish Macbeth,' said Jimmy. 'That bastard's going to pay for this with his life.'

Hamish went through to their little hotel sitting room the following morning. Olivia looked up at him, her face shiny bright as if lacquered. He thought, She's going to say, 'I hope you are not going to take what happened between us last night seriously.'

'Sit down, Hamish. Coffee? There's something we need to discuss.'

'You're going to say that last night is to be forgotten,' said Hamish.

'Well, yes. We've got a job on and we cannot have any emotional involvement.'

'Very well, ma'am.'

There was an awkward silence. Hamish switched on the television. It was the local news. 'A body was recovered from the harbour at Strathbane this morning,' said the announcer. 'Police are not revealing the identity of the dead man until relatives have been informed. Foul play is suspected.'

'Find out who that was,' said Hamish.

'Why?'

'We're involved in a drug scam and suddenly there's a dead body. I'd like to know who it is.'

Olivia phoned Daviot, who said he would

phone back. 'I think we're both worrying too much, Hamish.'

'I've suddenly got a bad feeling,' said Hamish. 'Dammit, I know there's something gone wrong.'

The phone rang, making them both jump. Olivia answered it, listened, said thank you and rang off. 'He was a small-time crook called Callum Short.'

'Could they get a photograph of him over here?'

'Why, Hamish?'

'Chust a hunch. Please, Olivia.'

Olivia rang again and asked for a photograph of the dead man. 'I hope you're not cracking up,' she said to Hamish.

'How did he die?'

'He was strangled.'

'I'm worried.'

'But why?'

'I'll tell you when I see that photo.'

Olivia had ordered breakfast but Hamish picked at his.

After an hour, there was a knock at the door. 'That'll be the photograph,' said Olivia.

She swung open the door.

Jimmy White's henchmen walked in. Both held guns. One said, 'You'll put on your coats and come with us. One movement, Macbeth, and we'll shoot her first in the stomach.'

They put on their coats. 'And look cheery

about it,' the taller of the two growled. 'One sign to alert anyone and she's dead.'

Numbly they walked downstairs. Outside, there was a long black car. The door swung open. 'In the back,' they were ordered. They climbed in. Jimmy White was sitting there, holding a small pistol.

'Where are you taking us?' asked Hamish.

'Shut your face,' said Jimmy.

The car sped on out of Strathbane. Hamish held Olivia's hand. How had they been unmasked? Was it something to do with that body in the harbour?

Then he realized they were heading for Lochdubh.

'You taking me home?' he asked Jimmy.

'Aye, we did some checking up on you. I've been up all night,' said Jimmy. 'Highland copper who loves the place. So you'll die there.'

'Man, everyone will know you killed us!' said Hamish. 'You'll have all the police looking for you.'

'I'll be on my way to South America tonight,' said Jimmy. 'And I want everyone to know I did it. Nobody messes wi' me. I was thinking of retiring anyway.'

The car cruised down to the harbour at Lochdubh. Hamish could see Jimmy's high-powered boat in the harbour.

'As I said, I checked up on you,' said Jimmy. 'You're supposed to be taking a wee holiday. So as part of your holiday, you're coming on a sail with me. You're the only copper in Lochdubh, so there won't be any more of the fuzz around. Nobody likes a policeman, so the villagers won't be much interested in what you do. But just in case you try to warn any of them, they'll be killed.'

He's mad, thought Hamish. Stark staring mad. And yet, he'll get away with it. Dump me and Olivia at sea and head off to France or Amsterdam and disappear.

The car stopped on the harbour. 'Get out,' ordered Jimmy. 'You men, keep the guns concealed, but shoot if you have to. Hughie –' to the driver – 'take this car away and lose it.'

Hamish got out of the car and then helped Olivia out. He took a longing look at Lochdubh. If I ever get out of this alive, he thought, I'll never leave the place again.

'Hamish!' He froze.

Angela Brodie was hurrying along the waterfront towards them. 'Get rid of her fast,' snarled Jimmy.

'Why, Hamish,' said Angela, coming up to him, 'you're looking very grand. Won the lottery?'

'No, charity shop,' said Hamish.

'You'll need to tell me which charity shop and I'll go there myself,' exclaimed Angela.

'I've got to go,' said Hamish, conscious of Jimmy's gun in his ribs. 'I'll call on you when I get back.'

Angela looked from one to the other. Why

didn't Hamish introduce her and why was that woman with him so white-faced and frightened?

'Your sheep are all right, Hamish,' she said. Jimmy was urging Hamish away from her.

'What about the black one?' asked Hamish over his shoulder. 'It's sick. I think it's going to be put down. See you.'

Another jab from the gun. Hamish and Olivia went down the stone steps to the large white cruiser which was Jimmy's boat. They were urged down into the cabin. 'Tie them up and let's get out of here,' said Jimmy.

'What are you going to do with us?' asked Hamish as their hands and feet were bound.

'Weight you down and throw you overboard,' said Jimmy. 'Like I said, I was going to retire and this will be my last great up-yours to the coppers. No one makes a fool out o' Jimmy White.'

He jerked his head to the two henchmen. 'No need to guard them. Let's go up on deck. The smell of police gets up my nose.'

'What went wrong?' Olivia said through white lips when she and Hamish were alone.

'Someone blabbed.'

'Who?'

'Someone at Strathbane.'

'You mean police headquarters? Surely not. Maybe someone recognized you.'

'I didn't go out of the hotel without my hat and dark glasses on. I took them off the day of

215

the picnic, but only for the picnic. There's a lot of drunkenness in the police force and they consort with their informers.'

'Whoever did this must have known we would be killed.'

'Maybe not. Maybe they thought that the whole business would be aborted and that we'd all be left with egg on our faces.'

'Hamish, I'm terrified.'

He leaned forward and kissed her. It was all he could do. His mind went this way and that, but he could not see any hope for them. He was glad of the pain from the wire binding his wrists and ankles. It took his mind off, just a little, from his forthcoming death.

Then he cocked his head. 'Listen, another boat.' He listened again. 'Sounds like a fishing boat.'

'Ahoy there,' called a voice.

'Get your boat away, man. You're right across our bows.'

'I've run out o' baccy,' whined the other voice.

'Archie Macleod, by all that's holy,' said Hamish.

'Who's he?'

'Local fisherman. What's he doing out this time of day? And he doesn't smoke.'

'Should I shoot him, boss?' One of the henchmen.

'No, I'll give him a packet of cigarettes. Go downstairs the pair of you and keep them quiet. Don't want any shouts for help.'

216

'Bring your boat alongside,' yelled Jimmy.

'Verra kind of you, sir.'

Soon both engines were cut.

'You're going to a lot of trouble for a packet of cigarettes,' said Jimmy, eyeing the small figure of Archie Macleod with distaste. 'Here, take the whole packet and be off with you.'

The fishing boat drifted a little away.

'Och, I cannae reach,' said Archie. 'Boys, a bit o' help here!'

Suddenly fishermen came racing up the companion way of the fishing boat, seized grappling irons and pulled Jimmy's boat close to their own.

Jimmy struggled to get his gun out of his coat pocket, but Archie had also seized a grappling iron and with tremendous force for such a small man, he rammed it straight into Jimmy's chest and sent him sprawling on the deck. Archie leapt on to Jimmy's boat and held an evil-looking gutting knife to his throat, just as his two henchmen erupted on to the deck.

'They shoot us,' panted Archie, 'and afore the bullet hits me, you're dead.'

'Don't shoot!' shouted Jimmy, his eyes dilating with terror.

'Throw your guns in the water,' said Archie, kneeling on Jimmy's chest.

'Do as they say,' howled Jimmy, beside himself with terror. He had caused people to be tortured, killed and maimed but never in his unsavoury life had he himself ever been in such peril.

The men threw their guns in the water.

'Tie them all up,' ordered Archie. There was a splash as Jimmy's skipper left the wheelhouse and threw himself overboard.

'Silly man,' said Archie. 'He will not be getting far.'

Once Jimmy and the others were all trussed up, Archie made his way down to the saloon.

'Och, it iss yourself, Hamish,' he said cheerily. 'And your young leddy.'

'I wass neffer so glad to see anyone in my life, Archie,' said Hamish. 'Can you get this wire off? The lady first.'

Archie sawed at Olivia's bonds. 'You'll owe me a new gutting knife, Hamish,' he said. 'It'll neffer be the same after cutting wire.'

'I'll buy you a gold one,' said Olivia, and burst into tears.

'Dinnae greet,' said Archie. 'It's all ower. We got them all.'

When he and Olivia were free, Hamish massaged his wrists and said, 'How did you know?'

'It was herself, Angela, Mrs Brodie. You said something to her about a black sheep that had to be put down and herself kenned you didnae have a black sheep and she thought they looked a lot o' villains so she rushes into the Lochdubh bar shouting you've been shanghaied. Then she goes running around the

218

village, calling the folks out o' their houses. Man, I had a rare time. It wass like the movies.'

The boat began to move again. 'David Queen is at the wheel o' my fishing boat,' said Archie. 'He's towing us in.' Suddenly the sound of the engine cut.

'What now?' asked Hamish nervously.

'Och, he'll have stopped to pull the skipper o' this boat out of the water.'

Sure enough, there came cries and then the thump of someone being hauled on deck. Then the engine started up again.

'Davie Queen's been on the ship-to-shore radio to tell folks you're all right. Who's your leddy?'

'This is Detective Chief Inspector Chater from Glasgow, Archie.'

'My, my, imagine a bonny wee lassie like yourself getting mixed up with killers like thon! What you need is a nice man like Hamish here to marry and have some bairns. I wass chust saying the other day to the wife, it's time our Hamish got married.'

Hamish's face flamed scarlet. 'Drop it, Archie. You're a worse danger than Jimmy White.'

Olivia was standing on the deck beside Hamish as they approached the harbour at Lochdubh. The harbour was crowded. It looked as if the whole village had turned out.

A great cheer went up as Hamish and Olivia walked up the weedy stone steps to the harbour.

Hamish hoped he wouldn't cry. They were all there: Angela and her husband, Dr Brodie, the Currie sisters, minister Mr Wellington and his large tweedy wife.

Hamish went straight up and gave Angela a hug. 'You're a clever girl,' he said.

'I knew something was wrong when you talked about that black sheep,' said Angela, 'and your poor girlfriend looked frightened to death.'

For the first time in her career, Olivia felt reduced in status.

'We had better go straight to police head-quarters, Macbeth,' she snapped, 'after we have seen Jimmy and his associates taken away.'

Angela gave her a look of dislike. 'Who's she?' she asked Hamish.

'Detective Inspector Chater.'

'Oh, really? Doesn't the word "thank you" enter her vocabulary?'

Olivia felt ashamed of herself. 'I'm sorry,' she said to Angela. 'I owe you my life, and Archie.'

'You can thank them later,' said Hamish. 'Let's go to the police station and phone.'

'What happened?' cried Angela, and several voices added theirs to hers, demanding to know the story.

Olivia, who was still shaking with fright and nerves, could only marvel at the calm way Hamish told the story of their abduction. The crowd was silent, hanging on every word. Although she far outranked Hamish, she had to wait patiently, because this was Lochdubh, where Hamish Macbeth was king.

'We all know drug money corrupts,' said the chief constable heavily.

It was early evening. The table in the conference room at police headquarters was surrounded by top brass. Hamish and Olivia sat side by side at the end of the table.

'I cannot see how word could have possibly leaked out,' said Daviot. 'I think someone recognized Macbeth and told Lachie.'

'Who was Callum Short?' asked Hamish suddenly.

They all looked at him.

'The man who was strangled and thrown in the harbour.'

'Why?' asked Daviot.

'Because it is just possible he might have been the informant. It's just a hunch.'

Detective Jimmy Anderson was there. 'We checked up on him. He was a small-time villain.'

Blair stared at the table. He longed for a drink but there was only Perrier water. Thank God he had played his snouts close to his chest. He had destroyed the book with the names of his informants and had replaced it with a new record without Callum's name.

'I asked for a photograph to be sent to the hotel. Was it ever sent?'

'I'll find out,' said Daviot, and nodded to his secretary, who went out of the room.

'Despite all that, the operation has been a great success,' said Daviot. 'Jimmy White arrested and the others being rounded up.'

The representatives of the Glasgow police talked at length about how their troops were being massed for dawn raids on several addresses.

Daviot's secretary, Helen, came back in. 'Well?' demanded Daviot.

'The photographs and the file on Callum Short are missing,' she said.

'What about the computer log?'

'There's nothing on that.'

'What!' exclaimed Jimmy Anderson. 'There was first thing this morning because I looked it up myself.'

'This could mean that someone in head-quarters leaked the information about the scam to Callum and Callum tried to sell it,' said Hamish.

Blair could feel sweat trickling down inside his shirt.

'We'll need to start a full investigation,' said Daviot.

'If I could make a suggestion.' Hamish

222

Macbeth again. Blair suppressed a groan. 'If this Callum was selling information, then he would go to Lachie at the disco, and to get to Lachie, he would ask the bartender.'

'Hasn't the bartender been picked up?' asked Daviot.

Jimmy Anderson shook his head. 'He's disappeared.'

'Then we'll need to find out from the young people who were there if anyone answering Callum's description was seen in Lachie's,' said Olivia.

'We'll do that.'

When they were back in their hotel room, Hamish said flatly, 'I've a damn good idea who's behind the tip-off.'

'Who?'

'Blair. Detective Chief Inspector Blair. He's aye hated my guts and saw this as a way to get rid of me.'

'Surely not. But if those are your suspicions, you must tell Daviot.'

'Waste of time. He won't listen. Not unless I have some concrete proof.'

'There will be a thorough investigation. If Blair's guilty, then they'll get him.'

'Maybe, but I doubt it. He'll be covering his tracks all over the place. Well, we've got two weeks' leave. I'm going back to Lochdubh in the morning and then I'll start looking into Tommy Jarret's death again. Want to come with me?'

She hesitated and then suddenly smiled. 'I'd like that.'

'I don't think anyone they've arrested is going to say anything about Tommy's death,' said Hamish. 'They know they wouldn't last long in prison if they talked. Do you want anything more to eat? That buffet supper at headquarters wasn't very filling.'

'No, I'm all right. I'm very tired. I think I'll go to bed.'

Later they lay in their twin beds in the darkness. Olivia rubbed her wrists, which still hurt from the wire. She closed her eyes but terror seized her. She was once more in that boat, tied up, without hope.

'Hamish!' she wailed.

He came to her and got in beside her in the narrow bed and folded his arms about her. 'Hush,' he said. 'It's all right. Hamish is here,' and he cradled her like a child until she fell asleep.

In the morning, Blair sought an audience with Daviot.

'Good heavens,' said Daviot. 'You look a wreck.'

Blair was unshaven, his eyes bloodshot, and he looked as if he had slept in his clothes.

'I want your advice, sir,' said Blair humbly.

'Of course.'

'The fact is, sir, I'm having trouble with the drink. Och, why beat about the bush. I'm an alcoholic.'

'Are you sure? We all like our dram.'

'The pressure of work has been making it worse,' said Blair. 'There's this rehab in Inverness which can take me for six weeks to get me cured. I would like to go there as soon as possible.'

Daviot was touched. 'Of course you can go. You are too valuable an officer to lose. You were quite right to come to me. A lot of famous people are alcoholics and take the cure,' said the superintendent, naively convinced that there was a cure for alcoholism. 'Keep in touch with us about how you are getting on. I was going to discuss our investigations into how Jimmy White got tipped off, but I think you need a break from it all.'

'I do, I do,' said Blair fervently.

'And don't worry. Your whereabouts will be our secret.'

Blair thanked him fulsomely and left. He felt he had covered his tracks thoroughly. He had never discussed his snouts with anyone. He would suffer this damn rehab and keep his ear to the ground. One murmur that they had sussed him, and he would disappear.

Hamish began to fret about sleeping arrangements as he and Olivia travelled by police car driven by Kevin to Lochdubh. There was only one double bedroom. There was one cell with a bed in it, but he didn't much relish sleeping in it.

Kevin was silent and morose and, when they arrived at the police station, said curtly that he had better be getting straight back. He felt that he and Barry had been unfairly blamed for not keeping a close eye on Hamish and Olivia.

'Home at last,' said Hamish with a sigh. He led her through to the bedroom. 'This is all I've got,' he said awkwardly. 'I've got a bed in the cell I can use.'

She smiled at him, a wonderful smile.

'It's all right, Hamish. I won't turn you out of your bed. We'll share it.'

'Grand,' said Hamish, who felt like whooping and cheering. He put his suitcase on the bed and opened it.

'Hamish, you've brought all those expensive clothes back with you!'

'Aye, well, I feel I deserve them.'

'Thief!'

'No, chust taking advantage of a new wardrobe. I'll leave you to unpack. I thought we might have a bit of lunch and then call over on Parry McSporran.'

'The crofter who keeps the chalets?'

'Yes. May as well get started.'

Hamish went through to the kitchen. There was nothing to make a lunch.

'I forgot to do any shopping,' he called. 'When you're ready, I'll take you out for lunch.'

Half an hour later they walked along to the Napoli restaurant, Hamish stopping every so often to introduce Olivia to the locals. 'We'd best call on Archie Macleod sometime today and thank him properly,' he said.

They went into the restaurant. Willie Lamont was waiting table. In the heady days when Hamish had been promoted to sergeant before being demoted, Willie had been his police constable but had fallen in love with a relative of the restaurant owner, had married her and had left the force.

Hamish made for the table at the window. Willie, who was a compulsive cleaner, rushed to wipe the table. 'This will be that police officer you was kidnapped with.'

'Yes, this is Chief Inspector Chater from Glasgow.'

'So it isnae a romance, then?'

'Give us the menus, Willie, and push off.'

Willie handed them the menus. 'You have to watch out for Macbeth.' he said to Olivia. 'One christ after another.'

Olivia blinked.

'He means crisis,' said Hamish, who was used to translating Willie's malapropisms.

He looked at the menu. 'The veal escalope's good.'

'I'm a pasta junkie,' said Olivia. 'I'll have the linguine with the clam sauce.'

'Do we want wine?'

'Better leave it until this evening,' said Olivia. 'We'll do some shopping and I'll cook dinner.'

While they ate, Olivia went over and over again their ordeal on the boat. Hamish listened, knowing she had to talk it out. No victim support or therapy for us, he thought. We just need to help each other to get over it.

Then she asked him to tell her again all about the death of Tommy Jarret.

'The thing that still bothers me,' said Hamish, 'is why did he go to the Church of the Rising Sun? No drugs were found there. All the congregation seemed to talk about was sex. And yet he was searching from some sort of spiritual belief.'

'Some sort of religious belief?' asked Olivia.

'Not exactly. You know what they say, religion's for those who believe in hell and a spiritual belief is for those who've been there. Maybe you could get that girl Felicity to talk a bit more.'

The restaurant smells of good cooking were being replaced by a strong smell of disinfectant. 'It's late. We're the only customers now,' said Hamish, 'and Willie is making sure there isn't one germ left behind.'

'What's the time?'

'Three-thirty.'

'Already! Let's do some shopping.'

They left the restaurant and walked along to

Patel's, the general store. Hamish paid from a wallet stuffed with notes.

'Hamish,' said Olivia when they were outside, 'surely that's still some of the money they gave you to flash around when you were supposed to be a drug baron. You were supposed to hand over what was left or at least account for it on your expenses.'

'I'll think of something,' said Hamish.

After they had put the groceries away, they drove to Glenanstey. 'It's a grand day,' said Hamish, 'but it'll get dark quite soon now.'

'I find this landscape quite intimidating,' said Olivia, looking up at the towering mountains. 'It must be a bleak place in the winter.'

'We get some bad winters.' Hamish sounded defensive. 'But not as bad as they have further south. We're near the Gulf Stream up here. They even have palm trees down in Rossshire.'

'Nonetheless, I would miss the lights of the city.'

Hamish drove on in silence. He had a feeling that what that exchange had really meant was – Don't get any ideas, Hamish Macbeth. I am not going to live up here with you.

Parry's cottage was deserted. Hamish went up on to a rise and scanned the surroundings. No sign of Parry and his car was not outside the house.

'Let's see if the fair Felicity is at home,' he said.

Felicity opened the door to them. 'What now?' she asked.

'Just a chat,' said Hamish.

'Who's she?'

Hamish pressed Olivia's arm warningly. 'My girlfriend up from Glasgow.'

'So what is it?'

'I wanted to ask you a few more questions about Tommy.'

'I've told you all I know. My case comes up before the sheriff next week.'

'Look, can we come in?'

'If you must.'

She turned and walked through the kitchen and into the living room.

'I'm still interested in why Tommy went to that Church of the Rising Sun,' said Hamish. 'Tommy struck me as a bright boy and the people there were rubbish.'

'He said something about finding cults fascinating.'

'And that was all?'

'I s'pose.' Felicity shrugged her thin shoulders. The sun was going down and despite the cold of the approaching evening and the cold in the chalet, Felicity was wearing a scanty top and a long floating skirt of Indian cotton. But there was a sprinkling of gooseflesh on her thin arms. Hamish wondered if her parents had cut off her allowance and that was why she had not turned on any heating. But Parry would surely supply her with peat for the fire and not charge for it and yet the fire was unlit. Probably one of those people who considered heat a decadent weakness.

'I would have liked to see Tommy's Bible,' said Hamish.

'Why? Do you think there might be cryptic clues in Exodus, Sherlock?'

Hamish looked at her with irritation. That was exactly what he had been thinking, or that perhaps if Tommy had had any notes, they might be in the Bible.

'I find it odd it hasn't been found.'

'Look, would you shove off? I haven't anything more to tell you.'

'You might think of something,' said Hamish. 'Where's Parry?'

'How should I know?'

Hamish gave up.

Outside, he said to Olivia, 'We may as well try Parry later. There's a good tea shop down in the village.'

'I couldn't eat anything after that lunch.'

'We'll just have tea. Miss Black, who runs it, is very sharp. She might know something.'

As they got into the police Land Rover and drove off, Hamish could see Felicity's pale face at the kitchen window, looking at them.

'This isn't a village. It's a hamlet,' remarked Olivia as they drove into Glenanstey.

'And full of rude forefathers,' said Hamish.

Olivia surveyed the small huddle of houses.

'Why would anyone want to live here?' she marvelled.

'Because it's beautiful,' said Hamish testily. His little dream of himself and Olivia settling down at the Lochdubh police station was fading fast. 'Well, Miss Black likes it and runs a good business. Here we are.'

He parked outside the tea shop and they went in.

'You're latish,' said Miss Black. 'I was just thinking of closing up. But sit down. What can I get you?'

'Just tea,' said Olivia.

When Miss Black bustled back with a fat pottery teapot, milk and sugar and cups, she smiled at Olivia and said, 'The tea's real. No tea bags here.'

'Won't you join us?' said Hamish. 'This is Chief Inspector Chater from Glasgow. Although we are both officially on holiday, I'm still puzzled by poor Tommy Jarret's death.'

'Yes, it is puzzling,' said Miss Black, sitting down at their table. 'He was so young, so confident, although always talking about seeking the meaning of life and that's apt to rob anyone of their sense of humour.'

'Yes, there was talk of him being religious,' said Hamish. 'His Bible was never found and I wonder why. His parents would like it.'

'Oh, the Bible,' said Miss Black. 'He left it here the day before he died.'

232

Chapter Nine

This strange disease of modern life.
— Matthew Arnold

'Have you got it?' asked Hamish.

'No, I gave it to Mr McSporran.'

'When?'

'I took it over on my way to work, the day Tommy died. I was in a rush and I saw Mr McSporran in the lower field with his sheep and so I gave it to him.'

The door opened and two ramblers walked in.

'Excuse me,' said Miss Black, and rose to serve them.

'We'd better go and have a look at that Bible,' said Olivia.

'I don't understand.' Hamish shook his head in bewilderment. 'Why would Parry keep it and not say anything?'

'Maybe he did give it to Tommy, and who-ever killed the boy found it and took it away. I mean, you did say you thought there ought to be more of that book he was writing. So maybe they took that away and took the Bible as well.'

Hamish's face cleared. 'That must be it.'

Olivia frowned. 'You know Parry well?'

'Yes, we're friends. I usually drop in on him for a cup of coffee when I'm out this way.'

'Did not his choice of tenants strike you as odd? One junkie and one magic mushroom picker? Bit of a coincidence.'

Hamish darkened. 'It can't be anything more than a coincidence.'

'But wouldn't it be an idea just to ask him about a few things?'

'Aye,' said Hamish heavily. 'Let's go.'

Parry's car was once more parked outside his croft house. Hamish knocked at the door and Parry opened it.

'A few words,' said Hamish.

'Right you are,' said Parry cheerfully. 'It's all over the place about your kidnapping. This'll be that woman inspector I read about.'

'Yes, this is Olivia. We've just had tea at Miss Black's. Parry, she says she gave you Tommy's Bible on the morning of the day he died.'

Parry struck his forehead. 'So she did! Didn't I tell you?'

'No, you didn't. Why?'

'I'm telling you, that boy's death put it clean out of my mind.'

'So may we have it, please.'

'I put it out with the rubbish.'

'Why?' demanded Hamish.

'Och, like I said, I had forgotten it so I didn't want to be accused of keeping it so I put it in the rubbish, like I said.'

Hamish's heart was sinking by the minute. There was very little rubbish put out from a croft house. Food refuse went on to the compost heap. Paper was burned. But all Highland crofters were superstitious. None of them would burn a Bible.

'And when did you put it in the rubbish?'

'A couple of days ago.'

'Look, Parry. That was withholding evidence. That was *destroying* evidence.'

'But the case is closed!'

'You knew I had my suspicions about the lad's death. And what about the parents? Didn't you think they might have wanted their son's Bible?'

'It's no big deal, Hamish. Och, you're just showing off in front of the lady here.'

Hamish loomed over him. 'I'll be back, Parry.'

'Where are you going?'

'Neffer you mind, Parry. Come on, Olivia.'

'Where are we going?' she asked when they were in the Land Rover.

'We're going back to the police station to get a couple of powerful torches and we're going to search the council dump.'

'It'll be like looking for a needle in a haystack, Hamish!'

'I've got to try.'

'You know,' said Olivia, 'Parry's story did ring true.'

'Not to me. Any decent crofter would have got in touch with me and confessed to still having that Bible if he had genuinely forgotten about it.'

'So is there something fishy about him?'

'I can't think of anything but getting that Bible. There's Sean Fitzpatrick's cottage. He might lend us a couple of torches and save us going all the way home.'

Hamish climbed down and Olivia stayed in the Land Rover.

'What is it now?' grumbled Sean when he answered the door. 'I thought you might be getting over your adventures.'

'I wondered if you could lend me a couple of strong torches,' said Hamish.

'What for?'

'I'm going to search the council tip.'

'That should take you about a year. What are you looking for?'

'If you must know, a Bible.'

'A Bible? If it had been jewellery or money or something useful, I would have sent you to Crummy Joey.'

'Who the hell's Crummy Joey?'

'He's the chief scavenger. Searches the tip for valuables.'

'And where can I find him?'

'You'll find an old wooden fisherman's hut, right down on the shore near the tip. He lives there. But a Bible!'

'Have you got torches or not?'

'Oh, I suppose I'd better let you have them or I'll never get any peace.'

He turned and went into the house and came back with two torches. 'Return them to me in good order,' he said. 'And while you're at it, you might get me some spare batteries.'

'All right.' Hamish leapt into the Land Rover and gave the torches to Olivia.

He told her about the scavenger as they drove along. 'Not very hopeful,' said Olivia gloomily.

'It's a chance. Then we'll go back and grill Parry.'

Olivia suppressed a sigh. She had been looking forward to preparing a dinner for Hamish and going to bed with him.

'Why don't you report it to headquarters?' she said. 'They could get a squad of men out to comb the tip in the morning.'

'You forget, the case is closed.'

'But we're still heroes to them. They'd do it.' She took out her mobile phone. 'I'll call them now.'

'No!' said Hamish sharply.

She studied his face in the light from the dashboard and then she said quietly, 'You're

237

trying to find some proof before landing your friend Parry in it.'

'If we find the Bible by some miracle and there's nothing in it but scripture, then I'll return it to his parents and say no more about it.'

'You didn't even ask Parry about the coincidence of having two drug addicts as tenants.'

'I'll get to that,' said Hamish grimly.

At last the council tip outside Strathbane came into view in the moonlight, a wasteland of garbage above which the ever restless seagulls wheeled and dived.

'There's a wood shack over there,' said Hamish, pointing to a shed of a building on the shoreline. 'And there's a light on.'

He drove the Land Rover as near to it as he could. They climbed down and walked over the tussocky grass and then across shingle to the door of the hut.

He knocked on the door and called, 'Police. Open up!'

There was a shuffling of feet inside and then the door creaked open. A truly filthy old man stood there, illuminated in the candlelight from the room behind. He was clutching a packet of biscuits. His rags were covered in biscuit crumbs.

'What do you want?'

'We're looking for something you may have picked up on the tip.'

'I only get wee bits and pieces,' whined Joey. 'Why should I not pick up what folks are eager to throw away?'

'We're not accusing you of anything,' said Olivia soothingly. 'We only need your help.'

'Come ben.' He shuffled backwards into the malodorous hut which was crammed with old newspapers, odd bits of iron, pieces of china, biscuit packet wrappings, old tyres and various glass jars and bottles.

How long had he lived like this? wondered Olivia. His face was seamed and wrinkled and his eyes small and watery. The stink rising from his rags was choking.

'We wondered if you might have picked up a Bible,' said Hamish. He and Olivia stood. There was nowhere to sit down. There was a filthy mattress in one corner and one kitchen chair on which Joey now sat, staring up at Hamish, whose bright hair brushed the ceiling.

Joey shook his head. 'No Bible. And if I saw one, I wouldnae take it. Bad luck.'

His voice was faint and singsong.

Olivia went over and crouched down beside Joey's chair. 'We're really anxious to locate a certain Bible which was thrown away two days ago. We'd pay you for your help.'

He looked at her and smiled, exposing a mouthful of white false teeth. 'My, what a bonny lassie you are,' he crooned. 'How much?'

'A tenner.'

He struggled out of the chair and Olivia stood up and backed off. 'I can take you to where the latest stuff would be.'

'That's grand,' said Hamish.

Joey took up an old hurricane lantern and lit it with one of the candles which were stuck in wine bottles. Then he blew out the candles.

Unlike some council tips, this one was not locked, nor did it have a fence around it. With surprising agility, Joey trotted ahead with his lantern and soon they were stumbling over piles of garbage. The moon shone down and the seagulls screamed and dived. Frost was beginning to glitter on the piles of garbage. Olivia shivered and wished she had put on warmer clothes.

They reached a sort of road between the rubbish where the council trucks drove in. After about a mile of walking, Joey said, 'It'll be ower here, a bittie. And probably up on top.'

The latest truckloads had obviously run up a path and dumped their loads on top of the mountains of rubbish already there.

Flashing their torches, Olivia and Hamish and Joey began to search. After an hour, freezing with cold, and utterly miserable, Olivia could only admire the energy of Joey, who scrabbled away, humming under his breath. She had a sudden sharp longing for the busy streets of Glasgow, the buses, the shops, all familiar territory and, above all, where she was always in control, always in charge. Ever since the drug case began, she reflected, she had felt as if she were only some sort of female sidekick to Hamish Macbeth.

Another hour. Her clothes stank and her nostrils reeked with the smell of the tip. A seagull swooped down and screamed in her ear and she let out a startled cry, lost her footing and fell backwards into a pile of kitchen waste.

'Olivia!' called Hamish. 'Why don't you go back to the Land Rover and warm up?'

But the feeling that she might not be as strong or as tough as any man drove Olivia on. 'I'll be all right,' she said.

Her nose was beginning to run. Her eyes were beginning to run with the cold. And then she saw an edge of black leather binding. Laying the torch on the ground, she got down on her knees and scraped away the debris. It was a Bible.

Her voice croaking with cold and excitement, she shouted, 'I've got a Bible.'

Hamish scampered down from the top of a pile of rubbish. 'I'll hold your torch. Open it.'

With stiff red hands Olivia opened the Bible. 'Bingo,' she said. For on the flyleaf was written 'Tommy Jarret'.

'Let's go home and get changed,' said Hamish. 'We'll look at it properly at the station.'

They thanked Joey and Hamish handed him a ten pound note, which Joey tucked inside his rags and scuttled off. 'Look at him go,' said Hamish. 'Maybe that's the secret of a long life, all day out in the open air, never ruin your skin with a bath, keep your muscles supple by running up and down piles of rubbish. I wish I'd worn my own clothes. This lot's for the cleaners. Come on. Let's get out of here.'

When they returned to the police station, Olivia stripped off her clothes and put them in a canvas bag supplied by Hamish and soaked in a bath. After Hamish had a shower and dressed in fresh clothes, they went into the kitchen and stared at the Bible on the table.

'I'm almost frightened to look at it,' said Hamish.

They sat down and he opened it.

Tucked between the leaves of India paper was a folded piece of A4 typing paper. Hamish carefully spread it open on the table. His face grew grim as he read it. Olivia moved her chair round next to his and looked at it as well.

'I'm keeping this for the end of my book,' Tommy had written, 'in case Parry looks at my computer. He's in it somewhere, this drug business. Billy, a chap I used to share a flat with, met me one day in Strathbane. I told him I had given up drugs and just wanted to get away from it all. He told me about Parry, just said he'd happened to hear of this man out of Glenanstey who had chalets to rent. Parry seemed just a simple crofter. I'd suspected something might have been going on at the Church of the Rising Sun, but they were just a lot of daft folk talking about sex. I was at a loose end and wanted to take a break from writing, so I decided to follow Parry. I didn't think there would be anything there. I was just playing at detectives. Then one day, I saw him go into Lachie's. Nobody like Parry would have gone to Lachie's for any innocent reason. The next day when he was out on the croft, I looked in his cottage. There was an admiralty map of the area and there was a circle around the entrance to Loch Drim. Then two nights later, a car arrived. I saw Lachie get out with another man and they went into Parry's cottage. I went out and crouched down and peered over the window. Parry was showing them the map. I wanted to keep all this for the book but it's too heavy. I think they were plotting the landing of drugs. Everyone knows Lachie deals drugs. That's where I got the stuff anyway. It's too scary now. I'd better go to the police. But I feel bad. Parry's been kind to me. I'll tip him a warning. He probably just recommends safe locations along the coast.'

'Parry,' hissed Hamish. 'The bastard. Why did he do it?'

'Let's arrest the bugger and find out,' said Olivia.

* * *

243

Parry's cottage was in darkness. Hamish hammered at the door. After a few minutes, the lights went on. The door opened.

'Parry McSporran,' said Hamish. 'I am arresting you for the murder of Thomas Jarret. I must caution you that . . .'

'You're talking rubbish,' howled Parry. 'This is me, your friend.'

'We found the Bible at the tip.'

'So? I told you I threw it out.'

'There was a piece of typescript inside where Tommy described the visit you had from Lachie and, I assume, Jimmy White, and about Loch Drim circled on the admiralty chart and that he was going to the police but going to warn you first.'

Parry turned white. 'I neffer thought to look inside.'

At headquarters in Strathbane, the whole story came out in the interrogation room as the tape whizzed.

Parry had borrowed heavily from the bank to build the chalets and the bank was demanding he pay back the loan. He was in danger of losing his croft house. He had run into an old school friend, Hughie Grant, who was looking very prosperous. They had a drink and Parry had told Hughie about his troubles. Hughie said he could put Parry in the way of big money. When he heard it had to do with drugs, he refused. But the bank became even more pressing. He panicked. He went to see Hughie. At first it was storing drugs for them at the croft house and delivering them to certain locations. Then it was helping them to suss out locations to land the drugs. The bank loan was paid off. He told them he wouldn't be having any more to do with them but they told him the only way to retire from the trade was to die.

Then Tommy had come to him and told him he had found out about him and was going to the police but giving Parry time to make a break for it.

'It would have meant it wass all for nothing,' said Parry. 'I would lose my sheep, my house, my croft, everything. So I told Lachie. "Sit tight," he said, "and don't interfere."'

Parry said that two young men had called at Tommy's cottage on the day of his death. One was small, with a tattoo of a snake round one arm, and the other was tall and with his hair in a ponytail. Tommy's flatmates, thought Hamish. He had done nothing, as instructed. After a time, they left, and he went in and found Tommy dead. He had phoned Lachie. 'Call the cops,' Lachie had said. 'He's taken an overdose.'

Parry began to cry.

So much for me being a shrewd judge of character, thought Hamish bitterly.

* * *

Olivia and Hamish got to bed about ten o'clock the following morning and both fell instantly asleep, wrapped in each other's arms. Hamish awoke in the late afternoon. Olivia's hands were caressing his body.

'I don't have any condoms,' he whispered.

'I've got the coil. Do you have AIDS?'

'No.'

She raised herself on one elbow and smiled down at him. 'Then what are you waiting for, copper?'

Blair was sitting at an AA meeting in Inverness on Ness Bank. Outside the windows, the river flowed lazily past. The man behind him nudged him in the ribs. 'Oh,' said Blair, 'I'd rather just listen.' If you swine think I'm going to join you and tell you anything about me, you've got another think coming, he thought.

God, he could murder for a drink. But it was back in the minibus to the rehab. The man who had nudged him, Cyril, said, 'You know, if you want to get well, you're going to have to speak up a bit.'

'Leave me alone,' growled Blair.

Once back at the rehab, he made for the public phone and phoned Daviot. He listened while Daviot told him of the arrest of Parry. Then Blair took a deep breath. 'Anything come of that investigation, sir?'

246

'We're still looking into it. Carry on with the cure.'

Blair went up to his room and sat on the bed and stared into space. Another success for Hamish Macbeth.

It was too much. He opened the window and looked down. He was two stories up but there was a drainpipe next to the window.

He shinned down it and softly made his way out of the grounds. Down the road was a pub called the Bell but known at the rehab as the Alkies Slip, because that was where some of them fell off the wagon.

Blair pushed open the door and went in. He ordered a double whisky. He knocked it back, feeling the warmth permeating his body. It was nectar. He was about to order another when he knew that if he did, it would lead to another and another and he wouldn't be able to make it back up the drainpipe. So he bought a half bottle over the counter and reluctantly made his way back to the rehab. It was all Hamish Macbeth's fault, he thought bitterly.

The speaker at the meeting had said that when he was drinking, he blamed everyone and everything for his troubles.

But Blair hadn't been listening.

Olivia was on holiday and she enjoyed her first few days playing house immensely. The weather was glorious, an Indian summer, and apart from a sad visit to Tommy's parents, she and Hamish had gone for walks, had gone fishing, made love and had eaten the meals she had prepared.

But then the weather had changed. Driving rain had blown up the long sea loch, clouds had covered the mountains, and Olivia began to feel claustrophobic and very far from home. For a few days she had entertained the dream of marrying Hamish. But now she knew she was a city girl to her bones.

She was sitting in the kitchen one morning, watching the rain smear the windows, looking out at a blurred view of damp sheep and wondering what to do. Her shrewd mind told her that Hamish was not in love with her, though he might think he was. He just wanted to get married. She had found a photograph of a beautiful blonde tucked at the back of his sock drawer, and from local gossip she gathered the blonde was Priscilla Halburton-Smythe, to whom Hamish had once been engaged. He had not thrown the photo away, only hidden it so that she would not see it.

She heard him coming back and went to put on the kettle. He had said he was going into Inverness.

He came in and kissed her and then fished in his pocket and took out a small velvet jeweller's box. 'For you. Open it.'

Olivia opened the little box. A diamond and sapphire ring winked up at her.

'Is this what I think it is?' she asked.

'I suppose I should have asked you to marry me first.'

Olivia snapped the box shut. 'Yes, you should, Hamish. I can't marry you.'

'Why?'

'You're not in love with me and I couldn't bear to live here.'

'I *am* in love with you.'

'Okay. Let's try this. I can't live here. I would expect you to get a transfer to Glasgow.'

'But I thought you liked it here!'

'As they say, it's a nice place to visit but I wouldn't want to live here.'

Hamish picked up the ring box and put it in his pocket. 'If that's the way you want it,' he said stiffly.

'I'm leaving today, Hamish. I don't think you're going to forgive me for this rejection. But you're not in love with me.'

'If you say so. Let me know when you're ready to leave.'

And that was that. Hamish drove her to Inverness to catch the Glasgow train. He would not unbend. His stiff-necked Highland vanity would not let him. He stood on the platform and watched the train pull out. She hung out of the window and waved, but he would not wave back.

Hamish drove the long road home, now tired and miserable. He had planned to go to Strathbane and see if they had got any further with investigating who was responsible for the leak but he no longer had the interest or the energy. He was sure the culprit was Blair, but Blair was a wily fox and would have made sure there was no evidence against him.

When he got back to the police station, which still smelled faintly of the perfume Olivia had worn, he phoned Strathbane and put himself back on duty.

An hour later, the phone rang. Hamish answered it. It was Jimmy Anderson. 'This is probably a load o' rubbish, Hamish, but there's a report of the sighting of a monster in Loch Drim.' Jock, thought Hamish, and the way I feel at the moment, I'll kill him.

'It looks as if you willnae be promoted down here after all,' said Jimmy. 'Some bod from Amsterdam put in his expenses. Pieter something. Charged for giving the police a back-hander to look at some street videos to find out where you'd gone and you were shacked up with a tart. Daviot's a puritan. You've to report to the hospital for an AIDS test. Also, you'd better account for all that money they lent you to play the big shot. And what about the fancy gear?'

'I sent back the Rolex, the credit cards, passport, and the sunglasses, cuff links, all that stuff.'

'And what about the clothes?'

'Got ruined during the investigation.'

'What! All of them?'

'All of them.'

'Well, I suppose you'd better get something out of it. Daviot says he'll make you up to sergeant again so you've got a wee promotion.'

Hamish's heart sank. 'Just so long as they don't send me some daft constable like last time. I mean Sergeant MacGregor over in Cnothan doesnae have a constable.'

'Bad luck, mate. I think auld Daviot feels you need a stern and upright constable to make sure you don't stray on to the primrose path.'

'What a day!' moaned Hamish. 'I'll go and kill the monster for you.'

As he drove towards Loch Drim, the clouds rolled back and the stars shone down. He kept telling himself that he was heartbroken but with each mile Olivia's face grew fainter in his mind. The whole drug case began to seem in retrospect like a fevered dream.

As he drove into Loch Drim, he noticed that Jock Kennedy's store was still open and that many cars and a coach were parked in front.

He parked alongside and went into the shop. It was full of people. Jock and Ailsa were busy selling Monster Toffee and small plush toys of monsters.

Jock looked up and saw Hamish.

Hamish nodded to him and turned and walked out.

It was hard to make a living in the High-lands. Jock was doing good business and giving a lot of people some harmless excitement. It would be a shame to stop it. He didn't care much about anything anyway. He climbed back into the Land Rover and drove off into the heathery darkness of the Sutherland highlands.

Some months later, Olivia sat in a doctor's surgery in Glasgow.

'Yes, I am afraid there is a definite lump there,' said the doctor. 'It may be benign but I think you should have a biopsy.'

Olivia sat rigid. Traffic hummed on the street below the frosted glass windows of the surgery.

'How soon?' she asked through dry lips.

'As I said, I'll get on to it right away. The sooner the better. Are you married?'

'No. If it is cancer, will I need to have the breast removed?'

'Perhaps, but they can do wonders these days in building up a new one.'

It would get round the station, thought Olivia bitterly. If she had cancer and if she survived, new breast or not, she would be dubbed One Tit Olivia until the end of time. Men were cruel.

When Olivia returned to her flat, she looked at the phone. She had an impulse to phone

Hamish but she fought against it. This was one battle she would need to fight on her own. If Hamish had really loved her, he would have followed her to Glasgow. He had never even tried to get in touch with her.

About the same time as Olivia had heard the bad news, Hamish strolled along the waterfront with Angela. He had finally told her of how he had proposed to Olivia and had been turned down.

'She told me I didn't love her,' said Hamish, 'and that turned out to be the case. I wanted to be married and have children.' He sighed. 'It would have been nice to have a wee bairn about the place. She was such a bonny, strong, healthy woman.'

'You make her sound like a cow,' said Angela. 'Strong, healthy woman, indeed! Anyway, don't give up hope.'

'I've still got the ring.' Hamish laughed. 'Who knows? It might come in handy someday.'

If you enjoyed *Death of an Addict*, read on for
the first chapter of the next book in the *Hamish
Macbeth* series . . .

DEATH OF A
DUSTMAN

Chapter One

Love in a hut, with water and a crust,
Is – Love, forgive us! – cinders, ashes, dust.
                                              – John Keats

They are still called dustmen in Britain. Not rubbish collectors or sanitation engineers. Just dustmen, as they were called in the days of George Bernard Shaw's *Pygmalion* and Charles Dickens's *Our Mutual Friend*.

Lochdubh's dustman, Fergus Macleod, lived in a small run-down cottage at the back of the village with his wife, Martha, and four children. He was a sour little man, given to drunken binges, but as he timed his binges to fall between collection days, nobody paid him much attention. It was rumoured he had once been an accountant before he took to the drink. No one in the quiet Highland village in the county of Sutherland at the very north of Scotland could ever have imagined he was a sleeping monster, and one that was shortly about to wake up.

* * *

Mrs Freda Fleming had recently bullied her way on to Strathbane Council to become Officer for the Environment. This had been a position created for her to shut her up and keep her out of other council business. She was the only woman on the council. Her position in the chauvinist Highlands was due to the fact that the ambitious widow had seduced the provost – the Scottish equivalent of mayor – after a Burns Supper during which the normally rabbity little provost, Mr Jamie Ferguson, had drunk too much whisky.

Mrs Fleming nursed a private dream and that was to see herself on television. Her mirror showed a reflection of a well-upholstered woman of middle years with gold-tinted hair and a pugnacious face. Mrs Fleming saw in her glass someone several inches slimmer and with dazzling charisma. Her husband had died three years previously. He had been a prominent businessman in the community, running an electronics factory in Strathbane. His death from a heart attack had left Mrs Fleming a very wealthy widow, with burning ambition and time on her hands. At first she had accepted the post of Officer for the Environment with bad grace but had recently woken to the fact that Green was in – definitely in.

She figured if she could think up some grand scheme to improve the environment, the cameras would roll. She firmly believed she was born to be a television star. Strathbane was much in need of improvement. It was a blot on the Highlands, a sprawling town full of high rises, crime, unemployment and general filth. But it was too huge a task and not at all photogenic. She aimed for national television, and national television would go for something photogenic and typically Highland. Then she remembered Lochdubh, which she had visited once on a sunny day. She would 'green' Lochdubh.

One hot summer's morning, she arrived in Lochdubh. The first thing she saw was smelly bags of rubbish lined up outside the church hall. This would not do. She swung round and glared along the waterfront. Her eye fell on the blue lamp of a police station, partly obscured by the rambling roses which tumbled over the station door.

She strode towards it and looked over the hedge. Hamish Macbeth, recently promoted to police sergeant, was playing in the garden with his dog, Lugs.

'Ahem!' said Mrs Fleming severely. 'Where is the constable?'

Hamish was not in uniform. He was wearing an old checked shirt and baggy cords. The sun shone down on his flaming red hair and pleasant face.

He smiled at her. 'I am Sergeant Macbeth. Can I help you?'

'What has happened to Lochdubb?' she demanded.

'Lochdubh,' corrected Hamish gently. 'It's pronounced Lochdoo.'

'Whatever.' Mrs Fleming did not like to be corrected. 'Why is all that smelly rubbish outside the church hall?'

'We had a fête to raise money for charity,' said Hamish. 'Who are you?'

'I am Mrs Freda Fleming, Officer for the Environment in Strathbane.'

'Well, Mrs Fleming, like I was saying, it's because of the fête, all that rubbish.'

'So why hasn't it been collected?'

'Fergus Macleod, that's the dustman, doesn't collect anything outside collection day. That's not for a couple of days' time.'

'We'll see about that. Where does he live?'

'If you go to Patel's, the general store, and go up the lane at the side, you'll find four cottages along the road at the back. It's the last one.'

'And why aren't you in uniform?'

'Day off,' said Hamish, hoping she wouldn't check up.

'Very well. You will be seeing more of me. I plan to green Lochdubh.' With that, she strode off along the waterfront, leaving Hamish scratching his fiery hair in bewilderment. What on earth could she have meant? Perhaps trees or maybe gardens?

But he had enough problems to fill his brain without worrying about Mrs Fleming's plans. Behind him and, he hoped, manning the police office was his new constable, Clarry Graham. Clarry was a lazy slob. He had never progressed from the ranks. He rarely washed and slopped around in a shiny old uniform.

Then there was the problem of the new hotel. The Lochdubh Hotel at the harbour had stood vacant for some years. It had recently been bought by a Greek entrepreneur, George Ionides. This meant work for the villagers and Hamish was glad of that, but on the other hand he was aware that a new hotel would take custom away from the Tommel Castle Hotel, run by Colonel Halburton-Smythe, whose glamorous daughter, Priscilla, had once been the love of his life.

He went into the police station followed by Lugs. *Lugs* is the Scottish for 'ears', and he had called the dog that because of its large ears. In the police station, the fat figure of Clarry was snoring gently behind the desk.

I should wake him up, thought Hamish, but what for? It's as quiet as the grave these days. Clarry had strands of grey hair plastered across his pink scalp and a large grey moustache which rose and fell with every somnolent breath. He had a round pink face, like that of a prematurely aged baby. His chubby hands were folded across his stomach. The only thing in his favour was that he was a good cook and no one could call him mean. Most of his salary went on food – food which he was delighted to cook for Hamish as well as himself.

Oh, well, thought Hamish, closing the office door gently. I could have got someone worse.

Fergus was in the middle of one of his binges, and had he been at home Mrs Fleming would have seen to it that he lost his job. But Fergus was lying up in the heather on the moors, sleeping off his latest binge, so it was his wife, Martha, who answered the door. Martha had once been a pretty girl, but marriage, four children and multiple beatings had left her looking tired and faded. Her once thick black hair was streaked with grey and her eyes held a haunted look.

Mrs Fleming questioned her closely about her husband and fear prompted Martha to protect the horrible Fergus, for what would they live on if he lost his job? She said he was a hard worker, and the reason he collected the rubbish only once a week was because he had one of those old-fashioned trucks where everything had to be manually lifted into it by hand. Mrs Fleming was pleased by Martha's timid, deferential air. She gave Martha her card and said that Fergus was to report to the council offices at eleven the following morning. 'We must see about getting him a new truck,' she said graciously. 'I have plans for Lochdubh.'

After she had gone, Martha told her eldest, Johnny, to take care of the younger ones, and she then set out to look for her husband. By evening, she had almost given up and was leaning wearily over the humpbacked bridge over the River Anstey.

She found herself hoping that he was dead. That would be different from him losing his job. She could get her widow's pension, and when the third child, Sean, was of school age, she could maybe work a shift at the new hotel if she could get someone to look after the baby. Mrs Wellington, the minister's wife, had challenged her with the unsympathetic, 'You must have known he was a drunk when you married him,' but she had not. Certainly he seemed to like his dram like a lot of Highlanders. She had met him at a wedding in Inverness. He had said he was an accountant and working over at Dingwall. He had courted her assiduously. It was only after they were married and he had moved into the cottage she had inherited from her parents that it transpired he had no job and was a chronic drunk. It also transpired he really had been an accountant, but he had seemed to take a savage delight in becoming the village dustman. Then she sensed, rather than saw, his approach.

She swung round, her back to the parapet of the bridge. He came shambling towards her with that half-apologetic leer on his face that he always had when he had sobered up between binges.

'Looking for me?'

'Aye, a woman from the council in Strathbane called. Wants to see you in Strathbane on the morrow.'

'Whit about?'

'Didnae say. She left her card.'

'You should've asked.' Fergus had become wizened with drink, although only in his mid-forties. He had a large nose and watery eyes and a small prissy mouth. He had rounded shoulders and long arms, as if all the lifting of dustbins had elongated them. It was hard for Martha to think that she had loved him once.

'I'd better go and see her,' grumbled Fergus.

Martha shivered although the evening was balmy and warm. She had a feeling the bad times were coming. Then she chided herself for her fancies. How could the bad times come when they were already here?

Clarry slid a plate of steaming bouillabaisse in front of Hamish Macbeth. 'Try that, sir,' he ordered. 'Nobody can make the bouillabaisse like Clarry.'

'Aye, you're a grand cook, Clarry,' said Hamish, thinking he would settle for fish fingers and frozen chips if only Clarry would turn out to be a good policeman instead.

But the fish stew was delicious. 'Did you ever think of going into the restaurant business?' asked Hamish. 'A genius like you shouldnae be wasting your talents in the police force. The Tommel Castle Hotel could do with a good chef.'

'It's not the same,' said Clarry. 'You go to them grand hotels and they would want ye to cut corners, skimp on the ingredients to save money.' He ate happily.

'There was a woman here from the council in Strathbane. Wanted to see Fergus.'

'The drunk?'

'Himself. Maybe you could do something for me, Clarry. I've tried, God knows. I'm pretty sure he beats that wife o' his. Go along there tomorrow and see if you can get her on her own, and tell her she doesn't need to put up with it.'

'Domestics were never my scene,' said Clarry, tearing off a hunk of bread and wiping the last of the soup from the bottom of his plate.

'You're a policeman,' said Hamish sharply. 'We don't leave wives to be battered by their husbands any more.'

'I'll give it a try,' said Clarry amiably. 'Now when you've finished that, I've got a nice apple pie hot in the oven.'

Fergus drove over to Strathbane the following morning in the refuse truck. He was dressed in his only suit, a dark blue one, carefully brushed and cleaned by his wife. His sparse hair was brushed and oiled over his freckled pate.

He could feel anger rising up in him against the villagers of Lochdubh. One of them must have reported him for something. He would try to find out who it was and get even.

And so he drove on, one sour little cell of blackness hurtling through the glory of the summer Highlands, where the buzzards soared free above and the mountains and moors lay gentle in the mellow sun.

In Strathbane, he parked outside the square, concrete Stalinist block that was Strathbane Council offices. He gave his name at the reception desk and asked for Mrs Fleming.

A secretary arrived to lead him up the stairs to the first floor. Mrs Fleming had commandeered one of the best offices. Fergus was ushered in. His heart sank when he saw Mrs Fleming. Like most bullies, he was intimidated by other bullies, and in Mrs Fleming's stance and hard eyes and by the very way those eyes were assessing him, he recognized a bully.

'Sit down, Mr Macleod,' said Mrs Fleming. 'We are to discuss the greening of Lochdubh.'

Fergus's now sober brain worked rapidly. This woman was one of those Greens. Very well. He would play up to her.

'I'm aye keen of doing anything I can to protect the environment, Mrs Fleming.'

'Splendid. Why then, however, did you not collect the rubbish piled up outside the church hall?'

'If you take a look down from your window, missus, you'll see my truck. It's one o' thae old ones with the sliding doors at the side.'

Mrs Fleming walked to the window, and he joined her. 'Now, I hae to lift all the rubbish into that myself. No help. I'm getting treatment for my back. I can manage fine if I keep to the collection day, which is Wednesday.'

Mrs Fleming scowled down at the old truck. Not photogenic.

She strode back to her desk. 'Sit down, Mr Macleod. That truck will not do. I plan to make an example of Lochdubh.' From beside her desk she lifted up a black plastic box. 'Boxes like these will be given to each householder. Waste paper, bottles and cans will be put into these boxes and not in with the general rubbish. Wheelie bins will be supplied.'

Fergus thought of those huge plastic bins on wheels. 'I couldnae lift those,' he protested.

'You won't need to,' said Mrs Fleming triumphantly. 'Your new crusher truck will have a mechanism for lifting the bins in. We will also put large containers on the waterfront at Lochdubh. One will be for wastepaper, the other for cans and the third for bottles.'

'But if they've tae put the cans and bottles and stuff in the black boxes, why will they need the extra bins?'

'So that they have no excuses for not separating their rubbish if they've got extra stuff. The hotels and boarding houses will need to use the larger bins.' She leaned forward. 'We are going to put Lochdubh on the map, Mr Macleod. How much do you earn?'

Fergus told her. 'We will double that. You are now promoted to Lochdubh's own environment officer. What do you wear while working?'

'Overalls and old clothes,' said Fergus.

'No, that won't do for the television cameras.'

'Television cameras?' echoed Fergus.

'Yes, when you have succeeded in making Lochdubh a model village, I will come with the provost and various dignitaries. Press and television will be there. You must have an appropriate uniform.' She looked at her watch. 'Now, if you will be so good, I would like you to wait here. I have a meeting with the other members of the council.'

Clarry, with his broad pink face sweating under his peaked cap, ambled up to Fergus's cottage. He knew Fergus had four children because Hamish had told him, and because it was the school holidays, he expected to see them playing around. There was a baby in a battered pram outside the door. He waggled his fingers at the baby, who stared solemnly back. Clarry knocked at the door.

Martha answered it and stepped back with a little cry of alarm when she saw his uniform. 'Just a friendly call,' said Clarry. 'Mind if I come in?'

'I'm just getting the children their lunch.'

The children – Johnny, ten years old, Callum, eight and Sean, four – were sitting round a table. They looked at him as solemnly as the baby had done.

'What are they having for lunch?' asked Clarry, his mind always on food.

'Baked beans on toast.'

Martha looked so tired and white and the children so unnaturally quiet that Clarry's heart was touched. 'You all need feeding up,' he said. 'You just wait here. I'll do the lunch for you.'

'But that's not necessary . . .' began Martha, but with a cheery wave, Clarry was moving off with the lightness and speed which makes some fat men good dancers.

He returned after half an hour carrying two heavy shopping bags. 'Now if you'll just show me the kitchen.'

Martha led him into a small narrow kitchen. 'Off you go and watch telly,' said Clarry. 'Food on the table in a minute.'

Martha switched on the television and the children joined her on the sofa. Clarry beat sirloin steaks paper thin and tossed them in oil and garlic. He heated garlic bread in the oven. He tossed salad in a bowl. He chopped potatoes and fried a mountain of chips.

Soon they were all gathered around the table. 'There's Coca-Cola for you lot,' said Clarry, beaming at the children, 'and Mum and I will have a glass o' wine.'

The children gazed at this large, expansive, friendly man. Johnny thought he looked like Santa Claus. They ate busily.

'I'm afraid we're costing you a lot of money,' said Martha.

'I put it on my boss's account,' said Clarry.

Under the influence of the wine and good food, Martha showed ghostlike signs of her earlier prettiness. But all the time, she was dreading her husband's return. Clarry talked about his days of policing in Strathbane while the children listened and Martha began to relax. Her husband could hardly make a scene with a policeman in the house.

After lunch, the children settled down in front of the television set again. 'No, no, that won't be doing at all on such a fine day,' said Clarry. 'Mum and I'll do the dishes and then it's outside with the lot of you.'

'Why did you come?' asked Martha, as Clarry washed and she dried.

'Just to say that if your man is beating you, you should report it,' said Clarry.

'He's not beating me,' said Martha. 'Besides,

say he was, I couldn't support the children. They'd be taken away from me.'

Clarry looked down at her fragile figure. 'That would not happen for I would not let it happen, lassie. That's the lot. Now let's see if we can give those kids of yours some exercise.'

Clarry improvised a game of rounders with a broom handle and an old tennis ball. The children ran about screaming with laughter. Martha felt tears welling up in her eyes. When had she last heard her children laugh?

'So that's settled then,' said Mrs Fleming triumphantly as the members of the council looked back at her, feeling as if they had all been beaten and mugged. In vain had they protested at the cost of the proposed scheme. Mrs Fleming had bulldozed her way through all their objections.

She returned to her office where Fergus was waiting patiently. She took a tape measure out of her drawer. 'Now I'll just measure you for that uniform.'

Fergus felt bewildered. He had double the salary, and not only that, he had a chance to bully the villagers. Not one can or bottle or newspaper should make their appearance in the general rubbish. He began to feel elated. The good times were coming. The thought of a drink to celebrate flickered through his brain, but he dismissed it. As Mrs Fleming measured and made notes, he felt increasingly buoyed up by his new status.

He, Fergus Macleod, was now an environment officer.

Martha, from the position of her cottage, could see part of the winding road that led into Lochdubh. She also knew the sound of the rubbish truck's engine.

'Dad's coming!' she shouted.

Clarry thought that it was as if the game of rounders had turned into a game of statues. The children froze in mid-action. The sound of the truck roared nearer. Then they crept into the house. 'You'd better go,' said Martha to Clarry.

'Remember, lassie,' said Clarry, 'I'm just down the road. You don't need to put up with it.'

She nodded, her eyes wide and frightened, willing him to go.

Clarry ambled off and turned the corner to the waterfront just as Fergus's truck roared past.

Fergus parked the truck. Martha went out to meet him. Her husband's first words made her heart sink. 'We're going to celebrate tonight.'

Celebration usually only meant one thing. But Fergus was more eager for his new job than for any drink. He carried a box of groceries into the kitchen. There was Coke and crisps and chocolates for the children. There was an odd assortment of groceries – venison pâté, various exotic cheeses, parma ham, bottled cherries and cans of fruit. Martha thought wistfully of Clarry's offering of steak.

'What are we celebrating?' she asked timidly.

'I am Lochdubh's new environment officer,' said Fergus. He proudly told her of his increased salary, of the new truck, of the greening of Lochdubh.

For the Macleod family, it was a strangely relaxed evening. Martha prayed that the children would not mention Clarry's visit, and, to her relief, they did not. They had become so wary of their father's rages that they had learned to keep quiet on all subjects at all times.

For the next few weeks it seemed as if success was a balm to Fergus's normally angry soul. He even chatted to people in the village. Clarry felt obscurely disappointed. He had been nourishing private dreams of being a sort of knight errant who would rescue Martha from a disastrous marriage.

Martha had never known Fergus to go so long without a drink before. She was still frightened of him, like someone living perpetually in the shadow of an active volcano, but was grateful for the respite.

Then one morning, flyers were delivered to each household in Lochdubh announcing a meeting to be held in the church hall to discuss improvements to Lochdubh.

Hamish, along with nearly everyone else, went along.

Mrs Fleming was on the platform. She was wearing a black evening jacket, glittering with black sequins, over a white silk blouse. Her long black skirt was slit up one side to reveal one stocky, muscular leg in a support stocking. She announced the Great Greening of Lochdubh. Villagers listened, bewildered, as they learned that they would need to start separating the rubbish into various containers. New bottle banks and paper banks would be placed on the waterfront on the following day.

'What's a bottle bank?' whispered Archie Maclean, a fisherman.

'It's one o' thae big bell-shaped metal bins, like they have outside some of the supermarkets in Strathbane. You put your bottles in there.'

'Oh, is that what they're for,' said Archie. 'Oh, michty me! Waud you look at that!'

Mrs Fleming had brought Fergus on to the platform. The other members of the council had suggested that a uniform of green overalls would be enough, but Mrs Fleming had given the job of designing the uniform to her nephew, Peter, a willowy young man with ambitions to be a dress designer.

The audience stared in amazement as Fergus walked proudly on to the platform. His uniform was pseudo-military, bright green and with epaulettes and brass buttons. On his head he wore a peaked cap so high on the crown and so shiny on the peak that a Russian officer would kill for it. He looked for all the world like the wizened dictator of some totalitarian regime.

Someone giggled, then someone laughed out loud, and then the whole hall was in an uproar. Fergus stood there, his long arms hanging at his sides, his face red, as the gales of laughter beat upon his ears. He hated them. He hated them all.

He would get even.

The following day Hamish strolled down to the harbour to watch the work on the new hotel. Jobs were scarce in the Highlands, and he was pleased to see so many of the locals at work.

'Hamish?'

He swung round. Priscilla Halburton Smythe stood there. He felt for a moment that old tug at his heart as he watched the clear oval of her face and the shining bell of her hair. But then he said mildly, 'Come to watch the rivals at work, Priscilla?'

'Something like that. It worries me, Hamish. We've been doing so well. They're going to take custom away from us.'

'They haven't any fishing rights,' said Hamish easily. 'That's what most of your guests come for – the fishing. And you don't take coach parties.'

'Not yet. We may have to change our ways to compete.'

'I haven't seen a sign of the new owner yet,' remarked Hamish.

'I believe he's got hotels all over Europe.'

'Any of your staff showing signs of deserting?'

'Not yet. But oh, Hamish, what if he offers much higher wages? We'll really be in trouble.'

'Let's see what happens,' said Hamish lazily. 'I find if you sit tight and don't do anything, things have a way of resolving themselves.'

'How's your new constable getting on?'

Hamish sighed. 'I thought the last one, Willie Lamont, was a pain with his constant cleaning and scrubbing and not paying any attention to his work. One new cleaner for sale and he was off and running. Now I've got Clarry. That's the trouble wi' living in Lochdubh, Priscilla. At Strathbane, they say to themselves, now which one can we really do without, and so I get Clarry. Oh, he's good-natured enough. And he's a grand cook, but he smells a bit and he iss damn lazy.' Hamish's accent always became more sibilant when he was upset. 'If he doesn't take a bath soon, I'm going to tip him into the loch.'

Priscilla laughed. 'That bad?'

'That bad.'

'And what's all this greening business?'

'It's that bossy woman. You weren't at the church hall?'

'No.'

'She is from the council, and she wants us to put all our rubbish into separate containers. There come the big bins.'

Priscilla looked along the waterfront. A crane was lifting the first of the huge bell-shaped objects into place. 'We don't like change,' she said. 'They'll rebel. They won't put a single bottle or newspaper in any of those bins.'

'Ah, but you haven't seen the green dustman yet. There he is!'

Fergus, resplendent in his new uniform, had appeared. He was standing with his hands behind his back, rocking on his heels, his face shadowed by his huge peaked cap.

'Heavens,' said Priscilla faintly. 'All he needs to complete that ensemble is a riding crop or a swagger stick.'

'I think that uniform means trouble,' said Hamish. 'Have you noticed that traffic wardens and people like that turn into fascist beasts the moment they get a uniform on?'

'A dustman can't do much.'

'He can do a lot in the way of petty bullying. The Currie sisters didn't give Fergus a Christmas box, and he didn't collect their rubbish until they complained to the council.'

'Well, there you are. Any bullying, they'll all complain to the council, and then it'll stop.'

'If that Fleming woman will listen to anyone.'

'What's her game? Is she a dedicated environmentalist? It said on the flyer that she was in charge of the council's environment department.'

'I think, talking of bullies, that she likes to find ways of spending the taxpayers' money to order people around. In fact, here she comes.'

Mrs Fleming drove along the waterfront while they watched. She got out of the car. Fergus strutted up to her.

Priscilla exploded into giggles. 'Would you believe it, Hamish? Fergus *saluted* her.'

Hamish laughed as well. The summer days and lack of crime on his beat were making him lazier than ever and dulling his usual intuition. He did not guess that Fergus's silly salute would make Mrs Fleming not hear one word against him, and so set in train a chain of events which would lead to horror.